LOVE
with me

A *With Me In Seattle* Novel

KRISTEN PROBY

Cover Art by:
Hang Le

Photography by:
Regina Wamba

Interior Design & Formatting by:
Christine Borgford, Type A Formatting

In loving memory of Henry and Lucy.

books by

KRISTEN PROBY

prologue

Jace

"You could have given me notice," Joy, my best friend of more years than I can count says from the passenger side of my little Audi as I drive us toward the party being thrown tonight for the hospital. "Do you know how hard it is to find someone to cover for me at the clinic in less than forty-eight hours?"

"I'm sorry, I thought I'd mentioned it before," I reply with a sigh. "You didn't have to come if it was a pain in the ass."

She huffs, then taps my shoulder, and I glance down at her. Those green eyes of hers smile up at me.

"I'm sorry for flipping you shit. It's been a week."

"Me, too."

"I'm seriously *so* proud of you, Jace." She reaches over to squeeze my hand. "Being named the head of cardiothoracic surgery in your mid-thirties? Dude, you're a rock star."

I smirk, but her words mean the world to me. Joy has been my best friend since my freshman year of undergrad. She's been with me through *everything*.

I pull into a circular driveway and give my keys to the young kid manning the valet, then Joy slips her hand through my arm, and we walk up the steps toward the party. "You look really pretty. I like this dress."

"It's my favorite," she says with a smile, looking down at the little red number she's wearing as we enter the ballroom. "And these heels will likely kill me, you've been warned."

I laugh and pass her a glass of champagne, choosing a bottle of water for myself. "Seriously, thanks for coming with me. You never let me down when it comes to these things."

"Getting dressed up is kind of fun," she admits and sips her bubbly. Joy is as tall as my shoulder in her heels. Her honey-brown hair is wavy and styled perfectly, and she has minimal makeup.

Because she doesn't need it.

She's pretty and funny, and she's the best friend a guy could ask for. Which is why we're *just friends.*

I don't need to fuck up a good thing with my libido.

"Also, I wouldn't miss this for the world. I'm surprised your family isn't here."

I shift on my feet, looking around the room. All of the board members are here with their spouses. Colleagues from my department. People I respect and admire.

"They would have come," I reply with a shrug, "but the family will have a private celebration next week. You're invited, of course. What made your week bad?" I ask as we make our way to a long table set up with a spread of finger foods.

"A guy brought a carrier full of mice into the clinic, and they all got loose. It was chaos. One of the little suckers was elusive for two days."

I laugh, picturing Joy chasing mice around her veterinarian clinic.

"It's funny now, but at the time? Not so much. What about you?"

"Busy," I reply with a sigh. "Very busy."

"Because you're the best cardiothoracic surgeon there is, proven by this shindig thrown in your honor tonight," she replies with pride in her voice. "Of course, you're busy. You should take a vacation."

I snort. There will be no vacation for me for the foreseeable future. With this promotion comes a *lot* more work. We're interrupted for the next two hours by colleagues and administrators, wanting to chat and network. Joy is intelligent and charming, another reason I take her to every formal function we have.

I'd be bored to tears without her.

"Congratulations, Jace," Mick Leamon, my medical director, says as he approaches with his wife, Elizabeth.

"Thank you, sir. You remember my friend Joy Thompson?"

Joy shakes Mick's hand with a smile, but he looks at me with confusion.

"Of course. Hello, Joy. Still nothing more than friendship here?"

"Oh," Joy says with a laugh, waving him off. "No, Jace and I are old friends. I'm proud to be his date tonight."

Mick relaxes with a smile and nods, slapping me on the shoulder with a wink.

"Good. Not that I can say this officially, but not having the entanglements of a young family will only benefit you in your new position as chief, Jace. If you thought we demanded a lot from you before—"

"I know," I reply, already anticipating what he is about to say. "I should just sell my house and live in my office."

We all laugh and settle into an easy conversation about the hospital, and the evening goes by quickly.

Exactly three hours after we arrived, after dinner and my speech and all of the well-wishes, Joy gives our it's-time-to-leave sign.

She pulls on her earlobe, Carol Burnett-style. It's our *safe word* for events like these.

Once we're settled in my R8, and I'm driving back toward her house, she sighs.

"Another successful event. Are you working tomorrow?"

"Bright and early," I confirm. "Tomorrow is full of routine surgeries. There shouldn't be any surprises. I also have a couple of meetings. How about you?"

"I have surgeries in the morning as well, and appointments in the afternoon. I'm on call tomorrow night."

"So, basically, I won't see you again until it's time to get dressed up for another frilly party."

She laughs and shrugs. "This is just what we do, especially now that you have a fancy new title. But I'm always around if you need me."

I WAS WRONG. Today has been anything but routine.

"His blood pressure is dropping," my lead nurse announces, and I know we're fucked.

"Clamp that," I order as blood continues to flow over my hands. "Stop this fucking bleeding."

"Yes, sir."

Maroon 5 is blaring through the speakers of the room, singing about maps. I love music while I work.

But now, it's distracting me.

"Cut the music," I order. My voice is hard, and I'm focused on keeping the man on my table alive.

Twenty minutes later, the heart monitor is a steady beep, signaling that he's crashed.

I step back and take off my mask. The room goes silent as the machines are quieted.

What the fuck just happened?

What was supposed to be a routine valve replacement turned into utter chaos.

"Time of death, 4:33 p.m.," I say at last. "I'll go out and talk to the family now."

"I'm sorry, Dr. Crawford."

I nod and walk into the scrub room, wash up, then make my way to the waiting room for a conversation that I absolutely despise.

"Mrs. Walters?"

"Can we see him?" the woman in her fifties asks. She's surrounded by her children and their spouses.

"Can you come with me, please?"

"Of course."

I lead the family to an empty room nearby, shut the door, and turn to six hopeful faces.

"I'm very sorry, but Mr. Walters didn't make it."

Tears. Anger. Anguish. Confusion.

It's thirty minutes of hell as I recount what happened in the operating room, and what I *think* went wrong. But no explanations are enough because it won't bring their loved one back.

"Mrs. Walters, I'm so very sorry for your loss."

IT'S ANOTHER HOUR before I can return to my office, shut the door, and stare out of the windows to the Seattle skyline. Mr. Walters was my last surgery of the day, and only the fifth time in my career that I've lost a patient under my knife.

I'm in the business of saving lives, and I failed today.

I brush impatiently at a tear on my cheek and reach for my phone. I don't want to go home to an empty house tonight. I'll make myself crazy.

But I'm not in the mood for my family. I love them, and they mean well, but I don't want to talk about it. I just want to *be*.

So, I text the one person in the world that I trust the most.

Hey, Joy. I need you.

one

Jace

"Dr. Crawford, Dr. Leamon has asked to see you in his office."

My nurse's face is impassive as she takes my charting laptop from my hands. She's tired. We're all exhausted after the seven-hour surgery we just came out of.

"Any idea why?" I ask.

She doesn't look up as she shakes her head. "No, sir, you know what I know."

"Thanks. I'll see you tomorrow." She offers me a wave, her eyes still on the task at hand as I walk down the corridor.

I stop by my office to shed my coat and stethoscope, then walk up a flight of stairs to the medical director's office.

"Hello, Mick," I say as I step into his space and close the door behind me.

"Jace," he says with a friendly nod. "Have a seat."

"What's up?"

He frowns and glances down at the open folder before him. Mick Leamon is a tall, fit man of sixty-three. His hair is shockingly white, probably from close to forty years' worth of surgeries.

He's also someone I've grown to respect and admire.

"I'm not going to beat around the bush, Jace. We have a clusterfuck on our hands."

"How so?"

"Do you remember a patient by the name of Manuel Walters from a couple of months ago?"

"He died on my table."

He nods, his expression grim. "That's the one. The family is suing you and the hospital for wrongful death."

My hands tighten in my lap, and my stomach clenches. I've never been sued for malpractice. I've never even been threatened.

This could tank my entire career.

"Mick—"

"I know," he says, holding up his hands in surrender. "I know that you went by the book and that the investigation will find that you didn't do anything wrong. I'm not worried about this."

"Well, I'm glad, because I'm sure as fuck worried."

"Seattle General has an excellent team of attorneys who are already working this case."

"Why aren't they here with us?"

His lips tip up into a smile. "Because I thought it would be more comfortable if we started this with a friendly conversation."

"Should I hire my own attorney?"

"I don't think so."

"Let me rephrase, if it was *your* medical license on the line, would you hire your own damn attorney?"

"No," he says without pause. "The hospital stands with you, as do I. The attorneys are representing you. I don't think you need more counsel, but that's always an option if hell freezes over and it comes to that."

I exhale and nod. "Okay."

"I'd like for you to meet with the attorneys on Tuesday at noon."

I frown. "Mick, I'm in surgery on Tuesday."

"No." He closes the folder and rubs his hand down his face. "You're not. Unfortunately, as of right now, you're on paid leave while the investigation is underway, until we can get this cleared up."

"For how long?"

He shrugs. "A month? Six? Hell, I don't know, Jace."

"*Months*?" I stand and pace the office that overlooks Puget Sound. "Jesus Christ, Mick."

"We need you here, Jace, so trust me when I say that we're doing everything we can to wrap this up quickly. In the meantime, I'll fly Sean Tiller out from Boston to cover your surgeries."

"I hate Sean Tiller."

"He's an excellent surgeon."

"And a pain in the ass."

"I won't argue there," Mick says with a laugh. "So, we'd best get this investigation wrapped up so you can get back into the operating room."

"I didn't do anything wrong that day, Mick."

"I know that, too." He's somber again, sympathy and concern in his blue eyes.

"The chief position—"

"Isn't going anywhere," he immediately assures me. "It's still yours, and we will just make do until you get back to work. Go get some rest, see your family, go to the movies. Go do whatever it is you do when you're not here, and I'll see you on Tuesday."

I stare at him for a moment, then nod once and march right out of his office to mine so I can grab my things before I hurry to my car.

But now I don't know what to do. I don't want to go home. I don't need to be in my head right now.

Joy.

I want to see Joy.

She was with me after Walters passed, so she already knows the story, and she'll have words of wisdom.

She always knows what to say.

Since the gala two months ago, and losing Walters, I've been spending more time with Joy—when we both have time away from our respective jobs.

Which isn't as often as I'd like, so it's not like I see her every day. But we've managed to squeeze in an evening or breakfast here or there.

I can't explain what's happening, other than I just can't stay away from her.

She's working today, so I drive right over. Her vet clinic isn't far from her home, and at this time of day, she should be just about finished.

I haven't been here in years. Joy's remodeled the waiting room with new tile floors, comfortable, grey chairs, and a coffee station with fresh-baked cookies.

She said the smell of the cookies covers up any of the unsavory odors from the animals.

She's a smart woman, my Joy.

"Fuck off."

I stop short, blinking and looking around the empty lobby.

"Be nice, Bill," Stephanie, the receptionist, says with a frown. "He swears."

"Fuck off."

I glance behind her to find a parrot perched in a large cage. "Pretty bird," I say.

"Shithole."

I can't believe it, but I actually laugh. This might be the worst day of my life, but Joy's bird is a kick in the ass.

"Is Joy here?"

"Yeah, she's finishing up an emergency surgery. Everyone else is already gone for the day, and I'm just waiting for her to finish so I can lock up and go."

"Is she alone back there?"

Stephanie cocks her brow like I just asked a stupid question. "No. She has a tech with her."

"Go ahead and lock up. I'll wait."

"Sorry, but I'm not getting fired for you."

"Fuck off."

I laugh again. "Bill has a bit of a potty mouth."

"Yeah, it's why he's here. His owner, who also had a potty mouth, died a couple of months ago. We can't rehome a parrot that swears like a sailor. So, it seems he's an office bird now, and he just insults the customers."

"He adds color," I say with a shrug.

"If you're going to wait, do you mind if I go in the back for a few minutes? I have some medications to organize."

"Go ahead," I reply with a nod, watching Bill, who ruffles

his feathers as Stephanie passes.

"Shithole."

"Do you like Stephanie?" I ask him softly. "I saw the way you watched her."

"Fuck off."

"Hey, I'm not judging. I mean, she's not my type, but she's a pretty girl." I sigh and lean on the counter. "It's been a shitty day, Bill."

"Shitty day."

"Yeah. Hey, I'm sorry about your owner."

"Shitty day."

"I bet that was a shitty day." I rub my fingertips into my eye sockets. "Jesus, I'm holding a conversation with a bird."

"It's kind of cute."

My hands fall, and I whirl at the sound of Joy's voice. "Hey." She frowns when she sees my face. "What's wrong?"

I glance around, but she shakes her head.

"I sent everyone except Becky, my all-night tech, home. I just need to check on my patient once more before I leave."

She leads me back to where all of the animals are kept. On a table in the middle of the room is a small cat with stitches in its side.

"Nice stitch work."

"Thanks," she says with a wide smile. "She had some complications from being hit by a car last week, but she should be good to go now."

Joy turns to her tech and rattles off a whole list of orders, her voice firm, hands steady.

Once we're alone, Joy rewashes her hands, then leads me into her office where she collapses into her chair and takes a deep breath.

"Okay," she says and reaches for her water bottle. "Spill it."

"I'm suspended indefinitely," I reply, and she chokes on her water. I hurry around the desk to pound her on the back as she sputters.

She wipes her hand over her mouth and then gapes up at me. "What did you just say?"

"If I say it again, you have to promise not to choke."

"This isn't funny." She frowns.

"You heard me," I reply and drop into my seat across from her. "Remember that patient that died on my table a couple of months ago?"

"Of course."

"His family is suing me and the hospital."

Her jaw drops, and she's still gaping at me.

"And while I'm under investigation, I can't work. They're paying me though, so there's that."

"So there's that," she echoes, nodding slowly. "No, fuck that. You didn't do anything wrong, Jace."

Her immediate and fierce loyalty is a balm to my bruised confidence.

"They know that, too," I reply. "It's all a formality. Honestly, if it had been my father on that table, I can't say that I wouldn't want to look into a wrongful death case."

"It doesn't bring him back," she insists.

"No, but if there was malpractice, it could prevent it from happening again."

"You're defending the Walters," she says incredulously.

"No, I'm not saying it's right. I'm pissed as hell. But, in their shoes, I don't know if I'd do anything differently."

She blows out a breath and stares at me. Her brown hair is piled on top of her head. She shed her white coat after surgery, and she's in baby blue scrubs.

For the first time since I met her, I wouldn't say she's pretty. She's fucking hot.

"What am I supposed to do with time off?" I ask, trying to distract myself from Joy and her sexy scrubs.

"You said you wanted to make some changes to your house. Now is a good time for that," she suggests. "And you could learn to play the piano."

I cock a brow. "The piano?"

"Sure. You have good hands. Might as well use them for something."

"Now you have jokes. My career is almost over, and you have jokes."

She giggles and shrugs one shoulder. My dick twitches.

"I have tomorrow off," she offers. "I'll hang out with you, and you can come up with a plan. I know this will drive you nuts."

Because she knows me, inside and out.

"You're not kidding," I agree.

"I'll make you dinner tonight," she says as she stands to gather her things. "And if you're really nice, you can sleep in my spare room."

But I don't want to sleep in her spare room. No, I want to sleep with *her.* Which means I have only one option here.

"Dinner will be great," I reply with a grin and follow her out to the lobby. "I'll go home, though. I have to clean some stuff up before you come over tomorrow."

"Suit yourself," she says with a shrug. She unlocks the front door to let us out. "Do you want tacos or lasagna?"

"Yes."

She laughs as she waves at Bill. "Be good, Bill."

"Fuck off."

two

Joy

"I have chicken parm in the slow cooker," I inform Jace as we walk into my house. "Sorry, no tacos or lasagna, but I made plenty."

"You always make too much," he says with a smile as he closes the door behind us. Before we can walk any farther, both Carl and Nancy come running to the door to greet us.

"You've added to your brood," Jace says, squatting to pet Nancy, a sixty-pound, eight-month-old English Bulldog. "And this one is missing an eye."

"Shh," I admonish him as I lift my sweet kitty, Carl, into my arms and nuzzle his head. He purrs immediately, smiling up at me. "Don't hurt her feelings."

"What's your name, sweet girl?" he asks the dog.

"Nancy," I reply for her, set Carl on the couch, and watch as he happily jumps onto the floor, barely limping despite missing one of his front legs.

"Why do you always give them people names?"

"Because they deserve the dignity of a name," I reply, leading him through the house to the kitchen. The house smells of tomato sauce and chicken, and it makes my stomach growl. "I mean, who wants to be called cupcake?"

"Not you, apparently."

"Yeah, don't ever call me cupcake."

"So noted." His grey eyes are full of humor, the emotion replacing the anguish I saw when he first arrived at my clinic. "Let's not talk about the hospital tonight."

"Why, whatever do you mean?" I ask, batting my eyelashes innocently. Jace grips my hair in his fist, pulls my head back, and smacks a loud kiss on my forehead.

"That's why I love you. How long do you have in the kitchen?"

"Twenty minutes, tops. I just have to boil the pasta and add cheese to the chicken."

"Great, that gives me plenty of time."

He dashes back to the living room and starts gathering Nancy's toys and throwing them into the box in the corner, but Nancy joins him and pulls them all out, one at a time as if Jace is playing a fun new game with her.

"Hey, I'm trying to clean up your mess," he says, making me giggle.

"She's pretty much a toddler," I inform him and turn to pull pasta out of the pantry. "And you don't have to clean my house."

"I always do this," he reminds me. "Why do you always have pants on your couch?"

I turn to watch him gather a pair of jeans off the arm of my sofa. "I'm not telling."

"Well, now you have to tell me."

"Sometimes, in the evening, I don't want to wear my pants anymore, so I take them off and drape them on the couch and forget to take them upstairs with me later."

He watches me with an expression that's new for him over the past couple of months. But before I can say anything, he just chuckles and walks to the stairs leading to the second floor. I can hear him bustling about up there, and then my washing machine starts.

Score. I don't have to do laundry later.

Since college, whenever Jace comes to my place to eat, he tidies up while I cook. He's a neat freak. I'm not.

Let me clarify. My house is not dirty. I'm a doctor, and cleanliness is important. Not to mention . . . ew. But I can be messy.

I think Jace feels useful, picking up after me. Or, he's disgusted by my clutter. Which could be the case.

"You don't have to do my laundry," I say as he comes into the kitchen a few minutes later.

"It only takes a minute to throw a load in," he says, immediately stacking the few dishes in my sink into the dishwasher. "Besides, I'm earning my keep."

"Your mama raised you right." I bump him with my hip, pushing him out of my way so I can reach for the pasta ladle to give the pot a stir. "You're better at laundry than me anyway."

"You'll always be a better cook," he says with a shrug and sets a clean mug in my cabinet. "We all have our strengths."

"True that. Okay, this is about ready. Do you mind reaching for the plates?"

Moving around my kitchen with him in it is easier than I expect it to be, every single time. The man is big, in the best ways. When I first met him in college, he was tall but lanky, still growing into his manhood.

And man, has he grown into it.

He's broad and firm, with muscles in all the right places.

Last week, we were at his house, and he dribbled some coffee on his shirt, so he whipped it off before going to fetch another one, and I'm pretty sure my jaw hit the floor.

Because hello, abs aplenty. Like, he has enough for about three people.

It's not fair.

"Why are you staring at me like that?" he asks, pulling me out of my ab-fog.

"I'm not staring at you," I lie, taking the plate from him and dishing up his food, then trading him for an empty plate to do the same for myself. "Do you want extra parmesan?"

"Duh." He reaches for the tub of shredded cheese and dumps it onto his pasta, then joins me at the table. Nancy immediately rests her chin on my thigh, waiting patiently for a handout.

"So, what do you want to do tomorrow?" I ask and take a bite of the chicken smothered in sauce and cheese, then let out a long moan of delight. "God, I'm hungry."

I glance up to see him frown, his fork halfway to his mouth.

"Well? What do you want to do tomorrow?"

"Whatever you want," he says, diving in for another bite.

"We could go browse through Pike's Market. Or go to the Pop Culture Museum. I heard they have a Marvel exhibit. Oh! We could take Nancy to the new dog park over by your house."

"Sure."

"To which one?" I lower my fork and study him. He's quiet, and he doesn't look at me. Of course, he's had a shit day.

"I'm fine with any of them, Joy. Honest."

I take a bite of pasta, then whip my scrub top over my head, tossing it onto an empty chair. I'm left in my white cami. "Cooking always makes me hot."

"I already put your laundry in."

My gaze meets his, and I'm surprised to find a little frustration and something else that I haven't been able to put a label on these past few weeks.

It can't be lust. *I'm* the one who's pined after Jace for years, not the other way around.

"It's okay, I'll do another load later."

He shakes his head and finishes the food on his plate, then carries it to the kitchen, rinses it, and stacks it in the dishwasher.

I slip a small piece of chicken to Nancy and laugh when she resumes her position on my thigh. I've taught her manners but haven't been able to break her of begging.

"Hey, I hate to eat and run, but I'm going to head out," Jace says, reaching for his keys. "Thanks for dinner. It was excellent as always."

"Okay." I swallow and frown. "Well, since we didn't decide on an activity for tomorrow, why don't I just meet you at your place at ten and we'll go from there."

"See you then." He shoots me a half-smile, waves over his shoulder, and walks out the door. I sit back in my chair, chewing my food, and reach down to pet Nancy on the head.

What in the world was that all about?

"SATURDAY," MY SISTER, Noel, says in my ear. I'm driving to Jace's house, and Noel has called with an *emergency*.

"I'm on call this Saturday," I reply.

"This is the semi-annual sale," she says as if that trumps my animal clinic. "We *have* to go."

"You can totally go," I insist. "Noel, the only reason I go is so I can buy something I don't need and get you more rewards points."

"Exactly. It's the last weekend for the sale, and we have to go."

"No can do, sis. Sorry."

She sighs heavily, making me smile. My sister is one year older, to the day, and my closest friend. We also couldn't be more different.

"Why are you so good at adulting?" she asks, disappointment heavy in her voice. "And why can't you have a regular job like the rest of us?"

"I've always been a bit different," I murmur as I turn down Jace's street. "You'll go find some cool things."

"But it won't be as fun without you," she says. "Let's get together for dinner one night, then."

"I can do that. Just text me."

I cut the engine, end the call, and frown at the red convertible Mini Cooper in Jace's driveway.

Shit.

Is this a booty call that hasn't left yet? Did he forget that I was coming over this morning?

He didn't sound particularly excited about hanging out with me today. Maybe he feels like I'm forcing him to go look at Captain America at the Pop Culture Museum.

"I'm so stupid." I groan and lay my forehead against the steering wheel. It's probably not a booty call. It's just a person.

Jesus, why am I always overthinking everything? Always.

I reach for my bag, lock the car, and ring Jace's doorbell.

"Hey, sugar," Wyatt, Jace's brother, says when he opens the

door with a smile.

"Hi there," I reply and walk right into his arms for a hug. Being best friends with Jace means that I'm close to his family, as well. "I've come to take Jace's mind off of serious things for today."

"Excellent," he says with a grin.

"Where is he?"

"I'm here," Jace says as he walks into the room, pulling a shirt over his head and giving me a peek at those lickable abs.

Damn.

I glance at Wyatt and connect the dots.

"Wait. Is that *your* car in the driveway?"

"Yep, I bought it for Amelia yesterday."

I frown. "Did you at least know that Lia wanted that car first? Or did you spring it on her? Because women still want a say in what they drive."

"She went with me." He glares at me. "You always bust my balls, Joy Thompson."

"It's what I do and who I am, thank you for noticing." I offer him a deep bow, making him laugh. "And I like the new car. It's super cute."

"She looks hot in it." Wyatt wiggles his eyebrows. "And I need to go pick up my fiancée so we can go to the florist and finalize the flowers for the wedding."

"How many days do you have left?"

"Six," he says immediately. "And it can't get here fast enough."

"You guys are adorable." I prop my hands on my hips and smile at him. "Aren't they, Jace?"

"The cutest," Jace says, smiling at his brother, who flips him the bird.

"On that note, I'm out of here." Wyatt says goodbye and leaves me alone with Jace.

"Good morning," I offer.

"'Morning. Do you need coffee?"

"Like I need air," I reply, following him into his kitchen where he already has my favorite mug waiting for me. It says: *Good morning. I see the assassins have failed.*

"It never gets old," I say with a chuckle as he pours the cream in, just the way I like it. "Thanks. Did you sleep at all?"

"A bit, in my office," he says, sipping his own coffee. "I was reading through the records again. There's just nothing there, Joy."

"Because you didn't do anything wrong." I walk up beside him, mirroring the way he's leaning back against the countertop, both of our arms folded, each of us drinking from our mugs. "The family is grieving, and sometimes the anger brings on something like this."

"Have you ever been sued?"

"No, but I've been threatened with it," I confess, and shrug when he stares down at me.

"Seriously?"

"Of course. When a pet dies unexpectedly, it's like a family member has died for many people. It's sad. But today, we're going to have fun."

"What did you decide on?"

"Well, first, I need to make sure that you *want* to do this. You didn't seem so sure last evening."

"I definitely want to."

"Okay. We're going skydiving."

He freezes. "Uh—"

"Kidding." I bump his hip with mine, making him laugh. "I

know you hate heights."

"You'll pay for that."

I smirk. "Sure, I will. You know what, why don't we just head downtown and we'll just make it up as we go?"

"Let's do it."

three

Joy

Downtown Seattle is bustling for a late Thursday morning. Then again, I don't think this city is ever truly quiet. Even on Sundays, there are races and other events happening, especially along the waterfront.

Jace and I walk down the sidewalk, just a few blocks up from the waterfront and Pike's Place Market, among throngs of people and shops, restaurants and offices. The city makes me feel energized.

We stop at a red light, waiting our turn to cross the street. When the signal turns, Jace takes my hand in his, linking our fingers to cross the road. He's done this before. He's a chivalrous guy.

When we safely reach the other side, I go to pull my hand away, but Jace tightens his grip, not letting me go. And I don't fight it.

"Let's go into Nordstrom," he suggests, making me laugh. "What? I want to look at their shoes."

"Seems I can't avoid Nordy's this week," I reply. "Noel called me earlier, wanting me to go to the semi-annual sale this weekend, but I'm on call."

"Awesome, *I* get you instead." He winks down at me. "How is Noel?"

"She's great. Busier than ever. Her business has exploded this year."

"Good for her," he says as he pulls the door of the store open, holding it for me, and my hand feels cold when I lose that connection with him. "So, the interior decorating business is thriving?"

"For her, it is," I confirm. "Lead the way. I have no idea where the men's shoes are."

"Do you know where *anything* is in here?"

"Can't say that I do," I reply with a laugh. "You know I'm not a shopper. That's Noel's department."

"I promise this won't hurt a bit," he says as he leads me to the escalator going down. This is the flagship store, and it's massive. A person could get lost in here.

The men's shoe section is bigger than most other department stores, and from the look on Jace's face, it's what dreams are made of.

"You might want to wipe the drool off your chin," I suggest, earning a tug on my ear.

"I love shoes," he says with a sigh, picking up a pair of tennis shoes. "I won't apologize for it."

"You have more shoes than I have hairs on my head." I lift a pair of Guccis, and about choke at the price on the sole, immediately putting it down before I ruin it and have to buy it.

Jace ignores my ribbing and proceeds to try on about six pairs of shoes before deciding on two of them. When he's finished, we return upstairs to leave, but the sunglasses catch my eye.

"I could use a new pair of these," I murmur as I start trying them on. "What do you think?"

"Are you trying to say, 'I'm Elton John's love child?'"

"No."

"Then they're not for you." He laughs and searches with me for another pair, his grey eyes moving over the glasses. He's in a black T-shirt and khaki cargo shorts. His arms flex as he reaches up to pull a pair down. "Try these."

"Hey, they're not bad." I turn my head, looking in the mirror. "You like?"

"Yes, ma'am."

"Sold."

"That was easy," he says.

"Why make it hard? I like them, and I hate to shop, so we're done here." I lead him to the customer service counter and pay for my glasses, and then we're off, back on the busy sidewalks of Seattle.

"Let's take these to the car and then get a bite to eat," Jace says. "In fact, you choose a place, and then I'll just run these to the car myself."

"I haven't been to the Palomino in a while." It's my favorite steakhouse in Seattle.

"That does sound good," he says. "Plus, we're parked near there, so it's perfect."

We rush the few blocks to the restaurant, which isn't busy yet, and are seated quickly. True to his word, Jace hurries over to stow our bags before returning to browse the menu.

"God, I don't think I've been here since we came to celebrate your birthday two years ago," he says as he sets his menu aside and takes a drink of his water.

"Same here," I reply, deciding on the steak frites. "It's so different at lunchtime versus the dinner rush."

"I like it," he agrees. "I can actually hear you."

The waitress comes with our drinks, takes our food order, and when she's gone, Jace reaches over to hold my hand again.

This is new. While Jace has always grabbed my hand to cross the street, he doesn't randomly hold my hand in other places.

It sends a tingle up my arm and straight to my nipples, making them pucker.

Jesus, I hope he can't see them through this thin, pink T-shirt.

"So, aside from the shoes you bought today," I begin, trying to distract myself from my suddenly uncomfortable breasts, and slide my hand out of his, "have you bought any other shoes lately?"

"Hmm." He spreads butter on a piece of bread and takes a bite, chewing as he thinks about it. "I found some new Jordans a couple of weeks ago. I downloaded an app on my phone that alerts me to new shoes so I can see what's coming and what I might want."

"Wow." I blink at him.

"Oh, it's a thing," he says and takes another bite. "There are people who even resell the ones that are hard to get. They make a ton of money. I guess if this surgeon thing doesn't work out, I could do that."

"No." I shake my head vehemently. "The surgeon thing is going to be fine."

"I could become a YouTuber and review shoes."

I continue to blink at him, and he finally dissolves into laughter. "You should see your face."

"I did *not* tutor you all through English Comp in college just to have you review shoes on YouTube."

"Hey, this isn't all about you."

"Yes."—I take a bite of bread—"it is. But it's an interesting hobby."

"What's your hobby, J?"

I stop chewing and frown at him. "Uh, work?"

"Nope, that can't be your hobby."

"Taking Nancy for walks."

He cocks a brow. "Bor-ing."

"Don't judge me, shoe-addict. I guess I like to cook, so that's a hobby."

"Okay, this I can work with."

"It's not about you."

He grins as his plate is set in front of him, his eyes never leaving mine. "Yes, it is."

"I BOUGHT APPLES, grapes, mango, and onions," I inform Nancy and Carl as I unpack my sacks in the kitchen. I've just walked through the door. Jace has gone home, probably to admire his awesome new shoes and find them homes in his ridiculously huge closet, and I'm looking forward to a quiet evening at home with my animals, a glass of wine, and Netflix. "Pike's Place Market has the best produce. Of course, they charge an arm and a leg for it, but it's totally worth it."

"Meow," Carl says before turning in a circle on the stool in front of the island and then beginning to take a bath.

"I know," I say as if I know exactly what he said. "The grapes *are* big. I think I'll freeze them."

Nancy follows me all over the kitchen as I wash and put away the produce. She has a doggie door to get in and out to do her business, but she really prefers to go with me during the day.

"I know, you've been alone all day," I say, giving her a scratch behind her ears. "Let's go for a walk."

At the word *walk*, she runs to the door and sits pretty by her leash.

"You're a good girl," I croon as I hook her up. She leads me outside, down to the sidewalk, and along the street. We always take the same route. I'm convinced Nancy could walk herself, she knows it so well. She stops here and there to sniff about, mark, and then rejoins me on the sidewalk.

Nancy is a happy dog. She's adapted well to having just one eye and living with me. In the beginning, I thought I'd foster her until we could find her a permanent home, but she bullied her way into my heart with her sweet, happy demeanor and funny antics.

She was meant to be mine.

When we come around the corner, only about a block from the house, I see that Jace's car is sitting in the driveway behind mine.

"I wonder if he forgot something," I say to Nancy.

"Rrrrfff," she replies.

"Or maybe he just missed you."

She looks up at me with a happy grin, that long tongue hanging from her mouth.

"Yes, I'm sure that's it."

We walk in to the smell of food and the water in the kitchen running.

"What are you doing?" I ask as I hang Nancy's leash by the door and walk into the kitchen.

"Your dishes," he says with a smile. "And I brought dinner. Oh! And these."

He hurries to the kitchen table and passes me a bouquet of flowers from the market.

"I didn't see you buy these."

"I went back for them," he says as if it's the most normal thing in the world. "I saw you sniffing them earlier."

"They're beautiful." I bury my nose in a hydrangea and breathe it in. "Thank you."

"You're welcome." He shuts off the water and wipes his hands on my towel. "I have burgers from Red Mill for dinner."

"It's not my birthday," I remind him.

He cocks his head to the side. "No, but you've got to be hungry. And I appreciated today. It helped more than I expected it would to keep my mind off of work. But if you're sick of me, I can take my burger home."

"I'm not sick of you." I roll my eyes and open the cupboard above the fridge, looking for a vase for the flowers. "I can never reach anything up here."

"Let me." He's behind me, his front pressed to my back as he reaches over me to retrieve the vase. "Here."

"Thanks."

It's a whisper. Every nerve ending hums, and I feel the loss when Jace steps away from me.

This is *insane.* Yes, I've been attracted to Jace for years, but it's never been like this.

"I was just going to watch some Netflix tonight," I inform him once I've got my voice under control. "You're welcome to stay."

"Burgers and TV? This is a treat." He grabs the bags of

food and follows me to the living room. "But is it going to be something mushy? Because you know how I feel about that."

"I was going to start bingeing something new, but I hadn't decided on what."

We eat and comb through the menu on the TV and decide on *Ozark*. Our bellies are full, our feet up on the coffee table. Carl's curled up in my lap, and Nancy is on the couch next to Jace, her head on his leg, snoring loudly.

It's as normal and domestic as it gets. Comfortable.

Easy.

My phone rings.

"It's Noel," I inform Jace before hitting the green button. Jace pauses the TV. "Hey, you."

"Did you go to Nordstrom without me?" she demands.

"How did you know that?"

"My assistant was there on her lunch break and saw you. I can't believe you went without me."

"I went with Jace. He wanted shoes."

"You didn't get *anything*?"

"Well, I did get new sunglasses."

She sighs heavily in my ear, making me chuckle.

"This is not funny!"

"It's totally funny. You sound like I slept with your boyfriend."

"Pretty much the same thing." I bust up laughing and glance at Jace, who is petting Nancy and smiling.

"I used your rewards card." I cringe, hoping this at least soothes her, and I'm not disappointed.

"Score," she says, happy again. "What are you doing?"

"Watching Netflix with Jace."

She's quiet for a moment, and I frown at the phone.

"Hello?"

"Have a fun night. Does Sunday work for dinner? We should invite Dad."

"That works."

"Okay, see you then."

I hang up and toss my phone on the coffee table. Before I can start the show back up again, Jace says, "Everything okay?"

"Noel doesn't love it when I shop without her. Probably because I *never* shop."

"She'll get over it." He takes my hand in his and kisses my knuckles as I hit play on the remote.

I'M LYING ON him.

I open my eyes and frown. The TV is off, but there's light coming in from the moon. Jace is on his back, lying down, and I'm *on him.*

My head is on his chest, and I can hear his heart. Our legs are tangled. And his arms are wrapped around my shoulders, holding on tightly.

I suspect Nancy is on her bed in the corner of the living room, given the snores coming from there.

We've slept like this before. In college, we'd fall asleep studying, and I'd wake up like this in the morning. It hasn't happened in years.

And I've *never* had the undeniable urge to rip off his clothes and have wild, sweaty sex with him. I've never let myself fantasize about him because, aside from Noel, he's my closest friend.

We're squarely in the *friend zone*.

I can't let anything happen to our relationship. And let's face it, sex just muddies everything up.

"Stop moving and sleep."

He shifts, drags his hand up and down my back, and kisses my forehead. He's warm, but not uncomfortably so. And my God, he smells so damn good. It's doing things to me.

"Sleep."

"I have to be smooshing you," I whisper. "I should move."

But his arms tighten.

"You're a little thing, Joy. You're not smooshing me. Now shut the fuck up and go to sleep."

I narrow my eyes. "You're bossy."

"Mm-hmm."

I sigh and stay where I am for about fifteen seconds until I can't stand it anymore.

"Seriously, I should—"

"That's it." He rolls sideways, pinning me between his big body and the back cushions of the couch behind me. "You're off me. Better?"

"What if I'm not sleepy?"

He kisses my forehead again and starts to push his fingers through my hair, rubbing my scalp and brushing the loose strands. Damn him, he knows I can never resist when someone plays with my hair.

"Oh, that makes me sleepy."

"I know," he whispers.

"You really do have good hands."

"It's part of the job," he says. "And all the better to play with your hair."

"I have little hands." I swallow hard. "I can't believe I'm about to admit this, but sometimes I worry that my hands are too small for surgery."

"Why?"

"Some of the animals I see are big. I'm strong, but I'm small, and I want the best for my patients."

"You are the best for your patients," he assures me. "You're the best there is, Joy. You're so fucking smart. And your heart is in it, and that's the most important piece of all."

"I know. It's what makes you a good surgeon, too."

"Is it?"

"Are you kidding me?"

His hand pauses in my hair.

"Jace, when your patient didn't make it, and you showed up here? You were devastated. I've never seen you like that."

"It's the first time that it was a shock that the patient didn't make it," he admits. "In the past, when I lost someone, we knew it was a possibility. It still sucked, but I knew it could happen. This one was different."

"And you *cared*. Do you know how many doctors would pay their respects to the family and then just get on with their day? A lot of them. People accuse surgeons of being heartless, and maybe sometimes they need to be. But you're not."

"It might be easier if I was."

I've missed this. Confessing our deepest thoughts in the dark. We haven't done this since college.

My hand glides up his side, over his shoulder, and I cup his cheek. He's let his stubble grow, and it's prickly against my palm.

"I'm proud of you," I say.

"I'm scared," he says. "I don't know what to do with this much time off. I *need* to work, not because of the money but because it's who I am, Joy."

"I know."

"I can work on projects at the house, and order all the damn shoes in the world, but none of that feeds my soul."

"You'll be back there," I assure him. "It might happen quicker than anyone thinks. Maybe the attorneys can talk the family into dropping the case, or the hospital will settle."

"We can hope." He sighs and tips his forehead to mine. "Thank you. For everything. But especially for this. You're the only one who gets it. You're the only one—"

He breaks off, and I want to know what he was going to say. I *need* to know.

"What?"

He shakes his head and takes a deep breath. "I don't know."

"What are we doing, Jace?"

He's quiet for a long moment, and I'm afraid I've taken this too far. But suddenly, he says, "Just sleep, Joy."

Our legs are still tangled. My arm is draped around Jace's waist, and he's cradling me to him, playing with my hair as my eyes get heavier and heavier.

"Okay," I whisper and give in to sleep.

four

Jace

Moving quietly isn't easy when you're six-foot-three, and the person you're trying not to wake up is tangled up with you.

Dawn is just breaking, casting the room in shadows. Joy's face is buried against my chest, and she's murmuring in her sleep.

She's a sleep talker.

I manage to disengage my legs and ease off the couch, replacing my chest with a pillow. Once I'm standing, I pause to make sure Joy continues sleeping.

Nancy snores from her bed, and Carl is curled up with the canine, both oblivious to me and my jumbled thoughts.

I grab my keys and quietly leave Joy's house. I need to go home. I need to get away from her and *think.*

I'm not sneaking off because I've done anything wrong. No, I just need to clear my head. To think things through and get a grip on these feelings I have for her. If I stayed on that couch for one more minute, I would have crossed a line I swore

I never would with Joy.

But it's becoming harder and harder to keep my damn hands off her.

"I'm a dick," I mutter and rub my fingers over my mouth. "I can't just leave her like that. This is *Joy*, not some one-night stand.

I've never even had a one-night stand, and I'm not going to treat Joy like one. This isn't the walk of shame. She's my best friend, and my fucked-up feelings can't mess with that.

She deserves better.

She's right, my mama raised me right, and respecting women is paramount to me. Sneaking off while she sleeps is *not* respectful.

It's fucking chickenshit.

So, I pull into a drive-through to pick up breakfast to take back to her. Yes, my feelings for Joy are changing, and have been for some time now. She's always been my friend. We're kindred spirits. But it's more than that.

She's more than that.

And it's messing with me, possibly more than the shit happening at the hospital is, and that's a lot.

I pull into her driveway, grab the bag of food and tray of coffees, and walk back into her house. She's sitting up on the couch, rubbing sleep from her eyes.

"I thought I heard you leave," she says quietly. "Thought you were sneaking out on me."

Guilty as charged. "Nah, I thought we needed more food."

"You feed me a lot."

I set the bag on the table and pass her a coffee, which she sniffs. She closes her eyes in happiness and issues a moan, making my dick twitch. Her hair is a mess, hanging around her face in loose, tangled curls. Her eyes are heavy with sleep, and her clothes from yesterday are wrinkled.

She's never been more beautiful.

"Complaining?" I ask with a laugh as I sit next to her on the couch.

"Of course, not," she says with a smile and reaches for her breakfast burrito, taking a big bite. Nancy, who has caught a whiff of the food, stretches and comes to beg at Joy's side. "These are so good."

"Mm," I agree, chewing. We fall into silence, eating and drinking coffee. What used to be a comfortable silence has turned into awkwardness. I can hear a clock ticking in one of the rooms. A car drives past.

And with every passing minute, I want to pull her to me and kiss the hell out of her. I want to peel off her clothes and tuck her under my body as I make love to her all fucking day.

But this is Joy.

"Fuck," she says, setting down her food and hanging her head in her hands. She pushes on her eye sockets, then scrubs her palms over her face. "We've made it weird. Why is it so fucking awkward?"

"I don't know." I stand, relieved that I'm not the only one who feels this way. I grab her hand and pull her into my arms, rocking us both back and forth. "And I'm sorry for it."

"I need you in my life, Jace."

"Hey, I'm not going anywhere."

Hell, no, I'm not going anywhere.

"But we'll start to avoid each other because who wants to sit in awkward silence?"

"It's one breakfast," I remind her. "You might be overthinking this just a tad."

"No," she says, pulling back so she can look up into my face. "You know what I'm talking about. It's been happening for weeks. I *know* you, inside and out, and things are changing."

"We're going to figure this out." I pull her to me again. Her body fits perfectly against mine. "We'll figure it out together. We're smart people. We've got this. The most important thing is, we're not *ever* going to lose each other, no matter what."

"Tell me you feel it," she whispers, her arms tightening around me.

"I've felt it for a long time," I admit softly, and we fall back into silence, just holding onto each other in the stillness. I don't know what else to say.

"I have to go to work," she finally murmurs into my chest. "I don't want to."

"I'm meeting with Levi at my place in a little while. He's going to help me with some of the projects I'm going to start around the house."

"That's nice of him."

Neither of us pulls away. I *love* the way she feels in my arms. Small yet strong. Feminine.

Sexy as fuck.

"I want to see you tonight," I say, and she sighs in my arms, then pulls away and pushes her hair out of her face.

"Jace, maybe we need some time apart. To think things through and figure out—"

"No way. I *know* I don't need any time away from you," I interrupt immediately. "Fuck that, Joy. I'm not running from this. I told you we're going to figure it out together, and that's what we're going to do. Not seeing you isn't the way to accomplish that."

She chews her plump lip and watches me with wide eyes, concern etched all over her beautiful face.

"I should be home around seven," she says at last, and relief rushes through me.

"I'll be here."

"THAT'S SIXTEEN FEET," Levi says a few hours later as he holds the tape measure. "This is going to be a lot of painting."

"I have a lot of time," I mutter, writing down the measurements. "Might as well paint this ugly bathroom. I think I'll get a new vanity, as well. And maybe new tile."

"Hire a contractor," Levi suggests. "Because tile is a bitch. You can afford it."

"Yeah, I'll hire someone for the tile. Wyatt will know someone."

Our baby brother's an architect and is hands-on when his homes are built. He has people for this sort of thing.

"Why isn't he here helping?" Levi asks. Levi is the eldest of us three brothers. He's a Seattle detective, and I couldn't be prouder of him.

"Because he and Lia are wedding planning. Again." I shrug. "He'll come help another day. We have to go pick up the tuxes on Wednesday afternoon."

"I know," he says. "This wall is nine feet."

"This is a big bathroom, considering no one ever uses it," I comment, looking around.

"This is a big house for one person," Levi agrees.

"It's an investment. And I love the view from the west side."

"Killer view," Levi says as he follows me out to the living room. He's casual today, in jeans and a T-shirt. His hair is cut short, and he's greying at the temples.

I'm quite sure his job is the source of the grey.

"What's your schedule over the next week?" I ask. "I could use some help around here. I'll pay in beer and titillating conversation."

"I have Sunday and Monday free this week," he says, then narrows his eyes on me. "You look tired."

"I'm fine."

He crosses his arms over his chest. "Not buying it."

"My job's in jeopardy," I remind him. "Not just my job, my fucking *life*. So, yeah, I've had some sleepless nights."

He purses his lips. "Nope, that's not it."

I drop my notebook on the couch and pace to the windows that look out past the city to the water then cross my arms over my chest.

"It's not supposed to be this way," I say at last. "She's been my best friend since I was nineteen. Through medical school, and internships. Through the death of her mom, and starting our careers and all of the shit we go through in life. It's *Joy* for Christ's sake."

I turn to Levi. He's sitting on the couch, one ankle crossed over the opposite leg, and he's watching me without judgment.

That's the best thing about Levi, he listens without judging.

"Over the past few years, we only see each other when one of us needs a date for an event. She's always my plus one."

"I know."

"But the last couple of months?" I shake my head and turn

back to the view. "It's different. I see her more often, and we connect even deeper than we did before."

"You've been in love with her for years."

I whirl at his words and stare at him, dumbstruck.

"You're not stupid, Jace. No other woman has stuck around because you always run them off. They're not Joy."

"Or, I just didn't want a relationship."

"Remember Allison Thorton?"

I cringe. "She couldn't cook worth shit. Her lasagna was awful. Joy puts . . ." My words trail off when Levi gives me a knowing look. "Point made."

"You've compared every woman to Joy whether you meant to or not," he says, and I laugh humorlessly. Because he's right. And no woman ever compared to Joy.

I think back over the past fifteen years and sigh. I've been in love with her since the minute she sat next to me in physics and introduced herself with the brightest smile I'd ever seen. Her brown hair was a mess. Her skin was perfect and smooth, and her eyes seemed to see right through me.

I was shy and dorky, and she didn't care.

"I don't want to lose the friendship."

"Who says you have to?"

"When I fuck this up, she won't want to be my friend anymore."

"So, don't fuck it up," he says as if it's the easiest thing in the world. I turn to him again, and he grins. "If it's that important, you work for it. You don't fuck it up."

"I think it might be the most important thing in my life, and a week ago, I would have told you that position belonged to surgery."

"Surgery doesn't love you back," my brother says soberly.

"And it never will."

I nod, shove my hands into my pockets, and swallow hard.

"You need to go for it," he continues. "Joy's awesome. We all adore her. There's no one better for you than her."

"I know." I take a deep breath. "I know it. I was already leaning that way because I'm having a *very* hard time keeping my hands to myself."

"Is she saying no?"

I think back on last night, the two of us on Joy's couch, me holding her close as we whispered in the dark, and I smile.

"No. She's not saying no."

"Well, there you go," Levi says with a nod. "Now, let's go shoot some hoops so I can kick your ass."

"You can try."

I NEED TO talk to her. I've thought about it all day, and that's what it boils down to. I need to sit down with her and put everything out on the table, explain how I feel, and ask her to tell *me* what's going on in that gorgeous head of hers.

We've always been good at talking. Communication isn't a challenge for us.

So, I'm on my way to her place. She should be home by now. We'll have dinner and talk through everything like mature adults.

I've missed her today. I spent the rest of the day with Levi, shooting hoops and buying paint, but my mind kept drifting back to the sweet woman with the bright smile and soft, honey-brown hair.

Jesus, I have it bad.

Anxious to see her, I jog up her steps and walk inside without knocking. We know the codes to each other's doors, and we *never* knock.

It's always been that way.

I intend to greet her normally and wait to touch her until we've laid our feelings out there, but when I walk inside, Joy is at her kitchen island, one hip leaning on the countertop as she thumbs through the mail.

Her hair is still in a knot on the top of her head. She's biting her lower lip. And her eyes brighten with happiness when she glances up to see me come through the door.

"Hey, you," she says, but I don't reply.

Fuck talking it out first. Every thought of communication flies right out of my head. The most important thing in this moment is getting my hands on her.

I stomp through the house, around the island, and with one hand on her hip and the other on her cheek, I lower my lips to hers.

She gasps in surprise, her eyes wide.

But she doesn't pull away, and I sink into her, our lips softening against each other. She sighs and buries her fingers in the hair at the back of my neck.

Jesus, she's sweet.

I boost her up onto the countertop and reach up to pull her hair down. I want the soft strands in my hands as I kiss the hell out of her.

She sighs as her hands drift from my shoulders, down my back, to cup my ass over my jeans.

Her legs are spread wide, and I'm pressed between them,

my hard cock snug against her hot core. I want to strip her bare and sink into her. I want to make her cry out my name.

I want to make her forget *her* name.

If I'd known years ago that it would feel like this with Joy, I would have made my move sooner.

My hands move back to her face, and I end the kiss, resting my forehead against hers as we both catch our breath.

"I came over to talk," I say when I can find my voice.

"That was a good conversation," she says and swallows hard, making me chuckle. "We should have more of those. They're important."

"I love your sassy mouth," I reply before covering said mouth with mine again and just drinking her in. I want her. Now. Here.

But we're not ready for that. And we really do need to talk.

"How was your day?" I ask when I pull away and smooth stray strands of hair off her face.

"I don't remember," she replies with a smile. "Kidding. It was fine. I delivered four puppies via C-section, and I only got peed on twice."

"Sexy," I say with a wink.

"It's good that I have a shower at work, along with several changes of clothes." She drags her fingers down my cheek. "How is Levi?"

"A pain in my ass."

"So, normal then."

I laugh and kiss her hand. "Yeah, he's good. I bought paint and kicked his ass playing some basketball."

"Are we painting your house?" she asks, blinking rapidly.

"Well, Levi and I are, yes. You're welcome to come help."

"Can I come supervise?"

"No, I'm the boss."

She smirks and jumps off the counter. "Right. Well, we'll see how long that lasts. I'm a very good painter, you know."

"No." I lean on the counter, watching her with my arms crossed and a grin on my face. "How did I not know that?"

"You think you know everything about me, Jace Crawford, but you don't. I still have some secrets."

And I look forward to discovering every single one of them.

"What's for dinner?" I ask.

"I was going to whip up breakfast," she says. "Omelet?"

"Perfect."

"I'm putting spinach in yours," she warns me. "You need more greens."

"Just when I was starting to like you, you make me eat spinach?"

"You like me," she says, her back to me as she looks for her omelet pan.

But she's completely wrong.

I'm head over heels in love with her.

five

Joy

"That dog just follows Dad all over the place," Noel says on Sunday afternoon. We're at Dad's, making dinner while he's outside with Nancy, working on the yard. "You should give her to him."

I stop peeling potatoes to turn and stare at my sister. "Uh, hello? She's mine."

"Okay, maybe you could share custody. Dad's been lonely, and Nancy clearly likes him."

I glance outside and grin at my one-eyed bulldog, who is currently sunbathing in the grass while Dad mows the lawn *around* her.

"Okay, that's pretty cute," I concede. "Maybe Dad would like to have Nancy around more. I could leave her here during the day when I'm working."

Our father isn't retired, but he works mainly from home, so maybe having Nancy here to keep him company isn't such a bad idea.

"Something to think about," Noel agrees, reaching for the hand-mixer. She's whipping up a batch of cornbread.

"Remember when you broke this?" she asks, pointing at the chip in the plastic of the mixer. "You were so mad, and you threw this on the floor."

"Yeah, I was mad at *you* because you raided my closet again and ruined my favorite jeans."

"Mom didn't even bat an eye," she murmurs softly. "She just told us to clean up our mess and that I'd be buying you new jeans."

"Which you never did." I turn to her. "Maybe you should go to that anniversary sale and make good on that."

She sticks out her tongue at me, making me laugh.

"These hand towels are threadbare," I say, trying to dry my hands. "Why doesn't Dad throw them away and get new ones?"

"You know why," Noel says softly. "Because they were Mom's."

She's right. Everything in the house is exactly the way it was the day Mom died. It's as if she's just run out to the grocery store and will walk back through the door at any minute.

"I understood it for the first year," I comment with a sigh. "I mean, we all miss her. But it's been two years now, and he hasn't made any changes at all."

"It's comforting for him," she says.

"It's not healthy," I reply and walk to the window to look out at Dad and Nancy, then frown at the third figure squatting in the garden. "Is that Jace out there?"

Noel joins me and nods. "Looks like it. Speaking of Dr. Handsome, you need to spill it."

"Spill what?"

Noel cocks a brow. "You're a smart woman, Joy. You know what."

I blow a raspberry through my lips and lean on the counter,

still staring outside as Jace stands and pushes the wheelbarrow full of weeds to the alley to toss the debris onto the compost pile.

"Things are changing," I say, watching his muscles flex under the weight. "Not in a bad way."

"I noticed you've been spending more time together," Noel says.

"We have, and honestly, it's been a lot of fun. I don't think I realized over the past few years that I missed him."

"Well, you've both been busy," she offers and pours her batter into a pan, then slips it into the oven. "But I feel like I need to point out that you never looked at him like *this* before."

"Like what?"

"Like he's a hot fudge sundae, and you want to lap up every drop."

I bust up laughing but don't deny it.

Because holy shit can the man kiss. I had no idea.

He might have ruined me for all other men.

But before I can say anything, both men and the dog come through the back door.

"What's so funny?" Jace asks as he walks straight to me and wraps me up in a hug. I haven't seen him since yesterday morning. I got called into work and spent all day there yesterday, and by the time I got home, I fell into bed and slept like the dead.

"Nothing," I lie. Jace narrows his eyes at me, but I change the subject. "What are you doing here?"

"Jace comes every weekend to help me out with the yard or things around the house," Dad says as he pulls two bottles of water out of the fridge and tosses one to Jace.

"You do?" I ask in surprise. I had no idea.

He leans in and whispers in my ear, "You don't know everything about me."

He's echoing my words from the other night, and it's hot as hell.

"Sometimes, we just watch sports," Jace adds, making my dad smile.

"I had no idea that you guys were such good buddies."

Jace squeezes my hand as if to say, *"I'll tell you all about it later,"* and Noel asks Dad where he put Mom's cornbread platter.

Nancy nudges my leg, wanting a scratch behind the ear, so I squat beside her and oblige.

"Hey there, good girl. Were you helping Grandpa in the yard?"

"She's an excellent helper," Dad says, and I scoff.

"Sure, she's excellent at napping in the grass."

"Well, that's her job," he says in her defense, and it softens my heart toward my father even more.

Larry Thompson might very well be the kindest, gentlest man ever born. The heartache he's been through over the last few years is just plain unfair.

When the table is set, we sit down for dinner. Nancy has abandoned my leg for Dad's, resting her chin on his thigh, waiting for a handout.

I love that she enjoys my father. Maybe I'll take Noel's advice and leave her with Dad once in a while if he's open to keeping her.

Dad slips Nancy a piece of chicken and rubs behind her ear before returning to his own meal.

Yeah, I don't think I'll have to talk him into it.

"Oh, girls, I have something for you," Dad says and jumps

up from the table. He hurries into his bedroom and returns with two small boxes. "I know your mother would want you to have these."

Dad hasn't given us *anything* from our mom since she passed, so this is a big deal. I hope it means that he's come to terms with losing her.

Inside my box is the heart-shaped locket that I bought for her the Christmas before she passed. Noel's is a charm bracelet.

We glance at each other, both surprised.

"Thanks, Dad," Noel says, setting the box next to her plate. "I know it's not easy for you to part with Mom's things."

"Well, I suppose I can't keep them forever," he says with a sigh, and again, Noel and I look at each other in surprise.

"If you'd like," I begin, "we would be happy to come over and help go through some of her stuff. We could donate her clothes to the women's shelter, and—"

"No." Dad's voice is hard, and his eyes have gone cold. My happy, jovial, good-natured father has been replaced by the grief-stricken one. "You will do no such thing."

"Dad," Noel says softly, "you just said yourself that you can't keep everything forever."

"You will not come in and take her out of here," he says adamantly. His hands have balled into fists on the table. "There's no need for that."

"Can we just tidy up?" I ask in desperation. "I mean, the dust rag she used is still on the mantle, ironically covered in dust."

"No," he says again and shakes his head. He won't look at either of us. He's gone pale. "No."

"Okay," Jace says and covers my hand with his. "It's okay, Larry. Now you know, that when you're ready, the girls will help. I'll help, too, if you'd like. I noticed you planted carrots out back. I don't remember seeing them last week."

And just like that, Dad takes a deep breath, rubs Nancy's head, and talks about his vegetable garden with Jace while Noel and I push our food around on our plates, half-listening.

When dinner is over, Noel and I clean up the dishes, and she makes a hasty escape. I can see the grief in her eyes as she waves goodbye and leaves out the front door.

Coming to Dad's house is never easy for either of us.

"I guess I should go, too," I say.

"Come to my place," Jace says. "I'd like to show you the progress in the bathroom."

"I have Nancy."

"She can stay here tonight," Dad says with a smile. Nancy is sitting next to his feet as if that's exactly where she belongs. "We'll watch some TV and make an early night of it."

"I'll come get her in the morning," I reply and give Dad a big hug. "I love you, Daddy."

"I know. I love you, too, baby girl."

"YOU HAVE TO talk to me," Jace says when we pull up to his house. I left my car at Dad's, and yes, I know what that means. That I'll be staying with Jace tonight. But it felt natural to just slip into his car and come home with him.

I just haven't said much because I'm way too inside my own head about my dad and Noel and Jace and all of the craziness going on in my life right now.

He throws the car into park, cuts the engine, and we walk

inside the house. He left a few lights on in the hallway and kitchen, and I walk directly to the wall of windows that frames the city and the Sound beyond it.

"I don't get it," I mutter as Jace joins me. He holds my hand, tangling our fingers. "How can he do it? How can he keep that house exactly the way it was when she was living?"

"He misses her," he says.

"Two years. She's been gone for *two years*, Jace. I miss her, too, but Jesus, it's been two years. There's no need to leave her dust rag out, or her laundry in the hamper. Her makeup on the vanity. My God, her hairbrush, full of hair, is still on the bathroom sink."

"Two years isn't that long when you've lost the woman you spent more than forty years with," he points out, bringing tears to my eyes. "I know she was your mom, and you were close, but Joy, she was his *wife*. His partner in all things. He slept next to her every night."

"You're right." I blink rapidly against the tears that want to fall. "I can't imagine it."

He squeezes my hand. "I know. I can't either. Why do you think I go see him every week? Because I know he's lonely, and I enjoy him. He's one of the best people I know."

"I can't believe you've been going to see him every week and I didn't know." I look up at him, then lean in and press a kiss to his arm. "You're a good man, Jace Crawford."

"Don't let it get out."

"Your secret is safe with me."

He smiles down at me, then tugs on my hand and leads me back to his guest bathroom. The trim is taped off, the floor and fixtures protected by a tarp, and the walls are covered in a bold blue.

"We got the first coat on today," he says. "Levi isn't great with a paintbrush, but he's an excellent taper."

"I love the color," I reply. "It would look fantastic with a Moroccan tile."

"I was thinking the same thing," he says with a smile. "Wyatt sent me the name of a good tile guy. I'll call him tomorrow."

I kick off my shoes into the hallway, pull my hair into a ponytail, and reach for a roller.

"What are you doing?" he asks.

"I'm starting the second coat." I smile over at him. "Might as well get this done."

"You don't have to paint my bathroom," he insists, but I've already poured the paint into the pan.

"I like doing this, remember?"

"Okay." He shrugs and reaches for another roller. But first, he sets his phone on the countertop and starts a playlist. Rob Thomas and Santana come blaring out of his phone, and my hips immediately begin to move as I roll the paint onto the wall.

"And it's just like the ocean . . ."

I shake my booty back to the pan to load my roller and find Jace watching me with a grin.

"What?"

"I like the way you move, Dr. Thomas."

I curtsey. "Thank you, Dr. Crawford."

I go back to my dancing and painting. After three more songs, Jace passes a glass of white wine under my nose, and I greedily take it from him, sipping it as I take in our handiwork.

"We're good at this," I say.

"You're good at everything," he replies, sipping his wine. Maroon 5's *Sugar* comes on, and with a half-smile, Jace sets our glasses aside and pulls me into his arms to dance.

"I love this song," he says.

Jace can do a *lot* of things well. He's amazing at math. He's the best surgeon on the West Coast, and maybe in the country.

And that's not just my bias talking.

But when it comes to dancing, he could give Fred Astaire a run for his money. He's light on his feet, his posture is perfect, and the way his muscles move as he sways makes my mouth go dry.

Jesus, he's a sight to behold.

I can't help but think that he'd move this way in bed, too—with confidence and grace. His hands are sure and strong, one on my back and the other holding mine as he moves us across the floor, making me laugh when he dips me back and then steals a kiss as he pulls me back up.

"You're charming," I murmur against his lips. "And this wine is going to my head."

"That was my evil plan," he admits and nibbles on the corner of my mouth. "Get you good and drunk."

"Hey, no hanky-panky," I inform him, jabbing my finger into his chest. "I'll stay in the guest room."

"Over my cold, dead body," he growls and buries his face in my neck as Adam Levine sings about girls like me. I have Jace wrapped around me and Adam in my ears, and it's a heady combination.

"Where will I sleep?"

"My bed," he replies immediately.

"I never said I would sleep with you."

"*Sleep*," he says. "Don't think for a minute that you're getting me naked."

I snort, making him grin.

"I mean, you must think very highly of yourself if you think I'll just take my clothes off and let you have your way with me."

He's barely moving now, just snuggled up against me, his mouth gliding over my skin as he talks, sending delicious chills over my body.

"I wouldn't dream of it." My voice is weak, and I feel him smile against me.

"There's no way I'd want to kiss you." He presses those lips against the pulse in my neck. "Bite you." He bares his teeth and nibbles me there. "Lick you."

He leaves a wet trail down to my collarbone, and I can't even remember what we were talking about now.

"Do you work tomorrow?" he asks, bringing me out of the sexy fog.

"No."

"Good." He presses his lips to my forehead. "You can sleep in tomorrow morning."

We spend the next thirty minutes cleaning up our painting mess, then gather our empty wine glasses and wander through the house to his master suite.

The room is massive with simple furniture and neutral-colored linens. More windows line the west window, showing off the city and the water beyond.

"I need a shower," I murmur, reaching high above my head in a stretch. Without a word, Jace marches into his bathroom, and then I hear the shower come to life.

"It's ready for you," he calls out. I walk to the doorway and lean one shoulder on the doorjamb, watching as he peels off his shirt, tosses it into his hamper, and disappears into the attached closet. Two minutes later, he returns wearing nothing but pajama pants and a smile. "Do your thing, babe."

He kisses my forehead and leaves me alone in the bathroom. He doesn't assume he can join me in the shower, and he doesn't ask. He just gives me space, and I'm grateful.

Because even though we've known each other for *years*, and have been through a lot together, he's never seen me naked, or vice versa.

And I'm a woman. I don't want the first time he sees me naked to be in the shower. The shower is sexy and fun, but it's not romantic.

I roll my eyes at myself, strip out of my clothes, and then get in the steamy spray, sighing when the hot water slides down my body.

I can't believe I'm here, in Jace's house, ready to be intimate with him. Because let's be honest, I'm *ready*.

I would have let him do me against the wet tile in the bathroom if he'd had the inclination.

"Didn't want to startle you," he calls out as he comes into the room. He can't see me through the foggy, glass shower door. "I'm just getting you some clean clothes."

"Um, thanks."

"They're on the counter for you."

And then he's gone again. That's Jace, thoughtful and kind, through and through.

I'd better watch myself because it would be incredibly easy to fall in love with him.

I pause with the soap in my hand and stare at the tile. Aren't I already in love with him?

No. I shake my head and rinse off. This is lust. He's hot, and I love him as a friend. We're attracted to each other, and we're just seeing where this goes.

I step out of the shower and reach for the towel to dry off, calling myself sixteen kinds of fool.

I'm lying to myself.

I reach for the clothes Jace left for me and smile. A Stanford T-shirt, our alma mater, and a pair of boxer shorts that are about five sizes too big. I roll them and pray they stay in place when I walk across the room.

It wouldn't be super sexy to have them fall around my ankles and trip me as I try to make it to the bedroom.

But I discover it won't matter in the least because when I return to the bedroom, Jace is sitting up in bed, his legs under the covers and just the sidelight on, but he's out cold, sleeping silently.

So, I slide into bed next to him and turn off the light. He eases down next to me, pulls me close, and then falls back to sleep.

Joy

S omething slides up my leg. I blink my eyes open and frown in the darkness. I'm not in *my* bed. Am I in a sleeping bag?

Jesus, is it a fucking snake?

A strong hand slips up the back of my calf, and everything comes flooding back to me. Not a snake.

"Jace."

"Mm," he murmurs, kissing his way up the inside of my leg. "Your skin is so fucking soft."

I can't reply. I've lost all my words as his mouth and hands move back down to my feet. He plants a kiss on the arch of my foot, and then digs in with his thumb, giving me the best damn foot massage of my life.

I knew he had good hands. I *knew* it. But holy hell, I really had no fucking idea how good.

And every inch of the bottom of my foot is directly connected to my libido. Screw reflexology, this is vaginaology.

He could make millions.

I sigh in sleepy happiness as he continues massaging my foot, my ankle, and up to my calf, then he pays the other foot the same attention.

"Middle of the night massages," I whisper. "I approve."

"I can't believe I fell asleep on you," he says, disgust in his deep voice. "I'm sorry."

"You're forgiven."

"That fast?"

I sigh as he kisses up to my inner thigh. "Uh, yeah. The foot massage was a nice touch."

"I didn't know you liked foot rubs." He nibbles my skin where his boxers meet my thigh. "Is it because you're on your feet so often?"

"Yeah, and because . . . *foot rub.*"

I feel him smile against my skin. I *love* it when he does that. I love that I make him smile.

"I'm going to take you out of these damn clothes," he warns me.

"I'll help," I offer, but he hurries to cover me with his big body, pinning me in place. He kisses my lips lightly, leaving me needy for more.

"Before we get naked," he begins, cradling my face in his hands. I can just make out his eyes in the darkness. "This is going to change everything."

"I know." I drag my fingertips down his cheek. "I know it is."

"Are you sure you want this?"

I swallow hard. "Are *you*?"

He sighs and tips his forehead to mine. We're silent for ten weighted seconds, and finally, he whispers, "I don't think I've been more confident of a decision in my life, and you know that I overthink everything."

I grin because he's right, I *do* know. It took him a good month just to decide on the duvet covering us now.

Jace doesn't make decisions lightly.

And we're exactly the same in that department. I'm not flighty or a fly-by-the-seat-of-my-pants kind of girl.

"As long as you promise that, no matter what happens, I won't lose our friendship, I'm in. Maybe you'll hate the sex."

"And maybe I'm the Dalai Lama," he quips, making me giggle. He nibbles the corner of my mouth, and shivers run down my arms. He drags his lips down my neck, and I sigh. "You're so responsive."

"You're good at this foreplay thing," I reply and let my fingers brush through the soft hair at the nape of his neck. He pushes the T-shirt up my torso, and I lift so he can pull it over my head. He tosses it onto the floor, and before I can fully register the cool air on my skin, his lips are locked over a nipple, gently sucking and immediately making my core tighten.

My toes are suddenly hooked in the waistband of his pajama pants, impatiently pushing them over his muscular ass. I want to feel *all* of him.

But rather than oblige me by getting naked, he turns his attention to my other nipple and glides his hand down my belly, under the waistband of the boxers I'm wearing, and doesn't stop until his fingertips hit the jackpot of my already wet center.

"Fuck," he whispers against my skin. "I could just touch you all night long."

"You'd drive me to insanity," I pant, suddenly finding it hard to catch my breath. "Let's go a little faster."

"No way," he says and kisses my belly with a smack. "You

said you liked my foreplay ways."

"And I'm *ready*."

"I'll be the judge of that."

He brushes the tip of his nose back and forth over my pubis and nudges his shoulders between my legs, opening me wide for him.

Why am I suddenly shy? We're in the dark, and I've known Jace for*ever.*

But we've never done this.

"Don't tense up now, sweetheart," he says and presses a sweet kiss just left of my labia. "You're stunning."

"I'm not tense," I lie. Rather than respond, he drags his tongue from my anus to my clit, making me arch my back and cry out, all nervousness flying out the window. Because all I want right now is Jace. All of him. Every part of him.

Right this minute.

I fist my hands in the sheets and hold on for dear life as he licks and sucks, fast then slow, taking me on the ride of my life.

My orgasm hovers over me. I can *almost* reach it, and then he pushes a finger inside me, and it's all over. I fall apart, writhing on the sheets, calling out his name.

Jace kisses up my torso and then leans over the bed to grab something from the side table.

Once he's suited up, he covers me once again, kissing me as he guides the head of his cock to my pussy. He presses just the tip inside and his lips to my ear.

"You're so fucking amazing."

I pull my knees back, opening myself wider to him, and urge him to press in farther.

"In me," I rasp. "Jace, I need you all the way."

He links his hand with mine, pins it above my head, and pushes in, balls-deep, making us both groan.

"Jesus, Joy. You're a fucking glove."

He pauses, giving me time to get used to his size. I shift my hips and rake the nails of my free hand down his back to his ass, gripping hard, and he picks up a rhythm, moving in smooth motions. His ass flexes in my hand, and I immediately decide that the next time this happens, it needs to be when I can see what's going on.

Because Jace's body is something to fucking write home about.

He's kissing and moving, and I'm trapped in the absolute ecstasy of being with him. It's beyond anything that I've ever experienced before, and I doubt that I ever will again.

He presses deep and groans as his orgasm overwhelms him, and when we're finally able to breathe somewhat normally again, he slips out of me, kisses me soundly, then rolls away and walks into the bathroom, turning on the light and letting it cast illumination into the bedroom.

He returns moments later with a warm washcloth, walking naked through the room.

Dear, sweet baby Jesus, he has a body on him. Clothes don't do him justice.

"Are you okay?" he asks softly.

"I'm great," I reply honestly as he cleans me up. "I could have done that."

"I woke you up," he says simply as if that explains everything. He finishes his task, then joins me under the covers, pulling me to him much like he had hours earlier, but this time, we're both naked.

And we just had sex.

I had sex with the best friend I've ever had.

"Stop overthinking it," he whispers before kissing my temple. "I've already done enough of that for the both of us."

"That did *not* suck," I admit, smiling into the darkness.

"So glad to hear it." His voice is heavy with sarcasm, making me giggle. His dick twitches against my ass, startling me.

"You recover quickly."

"With your sweet little body pressed to me? Fuck, yes." He kisses my neck, in a new spot that is apparently my ignition button because, holy hell, my nipples pucker again, and I can't resist grinding my ass against him. "Jesus, Joy."

"Are you tired?" I ask, biting my lip and praying that he says no because I'm ready for round two.

"I'm never too damn tired for this," he says immediately, rustling behind me. The next thing I know, he lifts my leg and slips into me from behind, and much to my surprise, round two is even better than one.

"I HAVEN'T SLEPT this late since I was a teenager," I grumble as Jace passes me a steaming mug of coffee.

"We didn't actually fall asleep until almost five," he reminds me. "We had to get *some* shut-eye."

"You do realize that I now have to do the walk of shame at my *father's* house to get my car? At almost noon?"

He just smiles and sips his coffee, watching me with happy, smug eyes.

"I'm not sorry," he says.

I climb into his lap, straddling him, and wrap my arms around his neck.

It feels so natural. So perfect.

"I'm not sorry either," I clarify before I kiss his forehead. "That's not what I'm saying. But he's my *dad*."

"Maybe he won't notice."

I stare down at him, blinking slowly. "Have you met my dad?"

He chuckles and kisses my cleavage. "Okay, he's going to notice."

I move to climb off his lap, but he clamps onto my ass, holding me in place. His fingers slide toward each other until they cover the crack of my ass over my jeans.

How is that the best thing I've felt in *ever*?

"I'm not ready to take you home," he admits, pressing up to grind his already-hard cock against my core.

"No?"

He shakes his head and licks my collarbone. "No."

"Well, it's already noon. What's another hour?"

His grin is full of mischief. "I love the way you think, Doc."

In one smooth motion, he flips us over, and I'm pinned under him, lengthwise on his couch. His fingers make short work of my jeans, and I pull his shirt over his head.

"Are we actually going to make it out of your house today?"

He smiles against my skin. "That's a fantastic new goal."

"SORRY WE DIDN'T come by sooner," I say to my dad much later in the afternoon. "We got hung up working on Jace's place."

Dad's grinning from ear to ear, standing on his front porch. Nancy stands next to him, happy to see me but doggy-smiling up at my father.

"Nancy isn't a problem at all," he assures me. "I didn't have her regular food here, so I shared mine with her."

"Which is why she's looking at you like you hung the moon," I reply with a laugh and call for Nancy to come down the porch steps.

She doesn't budge.

"Why do I think that you may have just lost yourself a dog?" Jace asks quietly, for my ears only. I frown up at him.

"I didn't."

I don't want to give up Nancy. She's a great dog, and I love having her companionship.

But watching her with Dad is just . . . *sweet.* Nancy nudges Dad's leg, wanting affection, so Dad squats next to her and kisses her head, scratching behind her ears and telling her what a good baby she is.

How can I take her away from him? It would be cruel.

"You know, Dad," I begin, "I love Nancy very much, but I've begun to worry that she spends too much time alone."

Dad's eyes are hopeful when he looks up at me.

"Is that so?"

"Yeah. She should have more companionship than I can give her because of my busy schedule."

Jace slips his hand into mine, giving it a squeeze.

He thinks I'm doing the right thing.

"Would you mind adopting her? I'm happy to bring over all of her things. She won't cost you anything, of course. I'll continue to cover the cost of her food and stuff."

Dad licks his lips, not able to look me in the eyes, and I know without a shadow of a doubt that I've done the right thing. He clears his throat.

"I suppose that would be just fine," he says, still looking down at Nancy. "She's sure a sweet girl."

"I know." I walk up the steps and sit next to Nancy, pulling her into my arms to hug her and whisper in her ear. "You take care of him, okay? I'll still see you all the time. I love you, sweet girl."

"Are you sure?" Dad asks as I stand.

"Absolutely. Nancy is clearly happy here, and I think you could both use the company. I'll bring all of her things over later today."

"Do I need to know anything about her eye?"

Sweet Nancy always looks like she's winking at you.

"No, she's all healed up. If it ever weeps or doesn't look right, just let me know, and I'll look at it. But she's as healthy as can be."

Dad pulls me in for a hug, surprising me. Mom was always the more physically affectionate one. "Thanks."

"You're welcome." I walk down the steps and expect Nancy to follow me the way she always does, but when I turn around, she's still sitting by Dad's side as if this is home and where she's supposed to be.

Because it is. I just didn't know it.

"By the way," Dad says before we can get into our cars. "It's about damn time."

"For what?" I frown up at him, but he just shakes his head and smiles.

"Youth is wasted on the young."

I glance over at Jace, who just shrugs and waves at Dad before sitting in his little sports car and firing the engine to life.

I do the same with my vehicle and drive to my house, which is only about ten minutes away. Jace follows, parking behind me in the driveway.

Without any words, I unlock the door and step inside. Carl comes running to the door, happy to have me home.

To my surprise, he looks behind me, searching for Nancy.

And for the first time, tears come to my eyes.

"I'm sorry, little guy, she's going to live with Grandpa." I sit with him and cradle him in my arms.

"Hey, are you okay?" Jace asks as he sits next to us and wraps his arm around my shoulders.

"Yeah, I'm silly. I'd grown really attached to that dog."

"Then why did you give her away? You could have gotten your dad another dog."

I shrug one shoulder and kiss Carl's cheek. "It wouldn't have been the same. You don't see a bond like that all the time, Jace. Dad and Nancy have something special. He's her human. Bringing her back here would have been cruel. She loves me, and she was happy enough here, but her home is with Dad. They'll be good for each other."

"I'm sorry it hurts you," Jace whispers and presses his lips to my temple.

"I'll be okay," I reply with a sigh. "I guess I was fostering Nancy, after all."

He tugs me to him and hugs me close. Carl wiggles out of my arms and walks over to Nancy's bed, where he curls up and takes a bath, which only makes me cry again because I'm convinced that he misses the dog.

In reality, he just loves that bed and needs a bath.

Or, maybe he misses her, too. Who knows?

I just know that *I'm* going to miss her.

seven

Jace

"Let me do this," Levi says as he fiddles with Wyatt's bowtie.

"My hands are shaking," Wyatt admits, taking a deep breath and looking up so Levi can fix the mess Wyatt made. "Why is it so hard?"

"Tying the tie, or getting married?" I ask with a grin.

"Both. We should have just gone to the Justice of the Peace and got it all over with."

"Right, because Mom would have been okay with that," Levi says.

"Not to mention Lia," I add.

"She has a whole camera crew here, taking photos and videos of her getting ready for her YouTube channel," Wyatt says with a proud smile. "She's not sharing the ceremony or reception, of course. But she thought it would be fun to share the process of getting ready with her followers."

"The women will eat that shit up," Levi agrees. "She's a smart woman."

"So smart," Wyatt agrees. "Do you have the rings, Jace?"

"For the sixth time, I have them," I reply.

Wyatt nods, and Levi finishes the tie, then pours all of us a shot of whiskey. "I think we could all use this."

"To Wyatt," I say, holding my glass in the air. We clink glasses and then down the shots. The whiskey burns down my throat, immediately making me feel warm and a bit calmer. I don't know why the hell *I'm* nervous. I guess Wyatt's rubbing off on me.

"Do you have the rings?" Wyatt asks me. Again.

I pat down my jacket, the pockets of my pants, and turn to Levi. "Do *you* have them?"

"No," Levi replies, laughter in his eyes. "I thought you did."

"Huh." I frown and pat my tux again, then look around the room. "I swear they're here somewhere."

"What the hell?" Wyatt demands, and Levi and I both laugh, fist-bumping each other. "That isn't funny."

"For the last time, I have the rings. I promise. I'm a doctor for Christ's sake, I think I can manage to not lose your wedding rings."

"Right." Wyatt takes a deep breath, then lets it out slowly. "I wish Amelia would let me see her before the ceremony."

"Isn't that bad luck?" Levi asks.

"Some people do that first-look thing for photographs. But Amelia wanted to wait."

"I think it's nice." I pat Wyatt on the shoulder. "And you're going to be great."

"Okay," he blows out another gusty breath and walks to his suitcase. He and Lia are staying here at the vineyard tonight before leaving for their honeymoon tomorrow. He pulls out a wrapped box and a card. "I have something for you to take to her."

"I'll be back."

I carry the box to the other side of the inn where the bridal suite is. Amelia's cousin, Dominic Salvatore, owns the vineyard. It's a beautiful spot for a wedding.

I knock on the door. "It's Jace. I have a delivery for the bride."

The door swings open to a flurry of activity. Wyatt wasn't kidding about the video crew. There are several cameras and even a boom mic in the room.

But more than that, there are about thirty people. Amelia's bridal party is small, with just her sister Anastasia and cousin Jules standing up with her. But she has a whole squad of women chatting and laughing, doing hair and makeup, and drinking champagne.

"Oh, Lia," Jules says with a smile. "You have a surprise."

I walk into the room and grin when Lia turns to me. She's in an absolutely gorgeous white gown. It's strapless with plenty of sparkle, and it hugs her curves down to her thighs before it flows out.

I'm sure the style has a name, but I couldn't say what it is.

"You're the most beautiful woman in all the land today," I say as I lean in to kiss her cheek. "My brother is a lucky son of a bitch."

She smiles widely, her eyes lighting up when she sees the wrapped box in my hand.

"This is obviously for you."

"Photographer," Anastasia says, looking around. "You'll want to catch this."

"This isn't for my YouTube channel," Amelia says to another

woman standing by. "Please don't record this."

"No problem."

She opens the card first, reading silently. When she gets to the bottom, she covers her mouth and sniffles.

"No crying," Jules says. "Your makeup is perfect."

"I know," Lia says with one last sniffle as she puts the card back into its envelope. "I'm not sharing that. It's too personal."

I smile, proud of my brother for finding a woman who has found the balance of living a public life and valuing the things she wants to keep close to her heart.

Lia pulls the ribbon free, opens the box, and the room gasps at the pair of diamond earrings inside.

"Fucking hell," Anastasia says, and the others nod in agreement. "Lia, those match your dress perfectly."

"Looks like I have the perfect earrings for today," Lia says with a grin and immediately turns to the mirror to pin them to her ears. They dangle and sparkle beautifully in the light.

"I'm so glad you're having an evening wedding," Jules says. "These earrings are going to sparkle like crazy."

Lia blinks rapidly, warding off tears, and reaches for another wrapped box and card.

"This is for Wyatt."

"I'll deliver it now. See you soon."

I wave to the ladies and hurry back to the groom's suite where Wyatt and Levi are laughing.

"Have you been drinking more without me?"

"Only one shot," Wyatt says. "What did she say? How does she look?"

"You choked her up, and she's wearing your gift today. She looks like a bride, and that's all you'll get out of me."

He smiles proudly, then frowns when I pass him the gift. "We weren't exchanging presents."

I roll my eyes. "Clearly, you both broke that rule."

He opens the card, reads it, and grins from ear to ear when he puts it away. But when he opens the gift, he gasps.

"What is it?" Levi asks just as our mom and dad walk into the room.

"A watch," he says, shaking his head. "A very expensive watch."

"Is she telling you that you're always late?" I ask, earning a slap on the arm from my mom.

"He's not late," she says and then kisses my cheek. "Oh, my boys look so handsome."

"You clean up pretty well yourself," I reply with a smile, tucking her into my side. "How's it going out there?"

"It's *beautiful*," Mom gushes. "Oh, my goodness, Wyatt, this wedding is just amazing. There are so many people bustling about, getting everything just so."

"Are you guys in here?" Joy asks, poking her head around the door. She rode with my parents, but I'll be taking her home with me later. "Sorry, I had to make a pit stop."

"Hey." I hurry to her, take her hand, and lead her into the room, excited to see her.

"This might be the fanciest party I've ever been to," she says with a laugh. "And trust me, this guy has taken me to plenty of fancy parties." She hitches a thumb in my direction.

"You are magnificent," I say, taking in her emerald green gown and black heels. Her hair is down, framing her face in loose curls. But it's her smile that always stops me in my tracks. "It's not right to be more beautiful than the bride."

"Now I know you're lying," she says with a laugh and moves in to offer Wyatt a hug. "Hey there, handsome. You look great. Are you nervous?"

"Nah, Levi's been feeding me whiskey."

"Levi!" Mom exclaims.

"What? It calmed his nerves, didn't it?"

"Don't worry, I'm done drinking," Wyatt says. "And we have fifteen minutes, so we should make our way out there."

"Let's go," Dad says, leading us through the inn and out to the area where they've set up about two hundred chairs for the ceremony. The reception will be held in a massive tent about a hundred yards away. It's already lit up, the tables set, and I can see several people bustling about inside, putting the finishing touches in place.

Dad escorts Joy to their chairs down in front. Joy is my date, *and* she's been close to my family for years, so she's sitting with Mom and Dad.

I'd have it no other way.

The guests are seated, with a few stragglers hurrying in to find their seats. But before long, the music starts. Levi walks in first, then I escort Mom to her seat and join Levi at the front.

Wyatt follows behind me, waiting nervously next to me as the music changes, and the girls start to make their way in.

Two little girls in matching white dresses drop rose petals down the aisle. Rather than make Stella and Olivia stand through the ceremony, they sit with their parents in the first row.

Jules walks in next, followed by Anastasia. The dresses they're in are the same color pink but different styles.

And, finally, the music changes once more, and everyone stands to see Amelia as she's escorted in by her dad.

I know this is especially exciting for Lia. Her dad had a massive heart attack last year. I performed the surgery that saved his life, and I'm happy that he's here to give his daughter away to my brother.

I glance over at Wyatt, who has tears in his eyes. He couldn't tear his gaze away from her if he tried.

And I can't blame him. I find Joy, sitting in the front row next to Mom, and smile when I see that she's watching me. I wink at her, and she winks back.

When Amelia and her dad reach Wyatt, the pastor asks, "Who gives this woman to this man?"

"Her mother and I do."

I'M AN IDIOT.

Joy is dancing, having the time of her life, and I see green.

Of course, it doesn't help that she's dancing with Will Montgomery. I've met him a few times since my brother became engaged to his cousin, and I can admit he's a nice guy. Very down to earth and friendly despite being the highest-paid quarterback in the NFL. He's happily married, and he and his wife are expecting their second child sometime after the new year.

But he has his hands on my Joy, and that makes me want to punch him in the face.

He twirls her out, then back to his body, making her laugh.

And I've had just about enough of that.

I set down my beer and walk onto the dance floor, tapping Will on the shoulder.

"Mind if I cut in?"

"Sure," he says with a grin. "Nice to meet you, Joy."

"You, too," she says as I pull her into my arms and move her around the floor. "Why did you do that?"

"Because I wanted to dance with you."

"But that was *Will Montgomery*. My favorite football player of all time."

"Yes."

She narrows her eyes at me. *"Will fucking Montgomery."*

"I've met him. He's happily married, you know."

"I don't care," she says, staring at me like I just told her, well, that Will Montgomery isn't a big deal. "I don't want to marry him, I just wanted to dance with him."

"And you did. Luke Williams and Leo Nash are here, too."

"I know," she says with a grin. "I'm too intimidated to talk to Leo Nash. Remember when I made you go to their concert when we were finishing our undergrad?"

"You didn't *make* me."

"They weren't your favorite. But you still went, and it was awesome."

"I'm sure Leo wouldn't mind if you said hello."

"But *you* would mind if I danced with him."

I shrug and brush a strand of hair behind her ear. "I'd rather be the only man touching you. Is that wrong?"

"No, I suppose not. If any of these girls tried to touch you, I'd cut them."

Her voice is completely calm, which makes it even funnier. I laugh and sweep her in a circle, enjoying the way she smiles smugly. As it seems it always is when she's within twenty yards of me, my dick is twitchy, completely aware that she's near.

I can't keep my hands off her.

Not that she's complained.

I cup her face in my hand and lean in to brush my lips over hers, lightly at first, then sinking in, claiming her in front of everyone.

"You don't have to worry about any of these women," I assure her. "I don't even see them."

"Wow," she breathes. "You did that here."

"I'll do it anywhere."

She swallows, then watches my mouth as I continue dancing her across the floor. "I guess I'm just surprised that you'd kiss me in front of all of your family."

"Why?"

"They'll ask questions."

"So? Let them. I don't have anything to hide. I'm not ashamed of you, Joy. You're the most amazing person in my life."

Her cheeks turn pink, and she smiles shyly, the way she used to when we were in school, and I'd tell her how fucking smart she was.

When the song ends, someone taps a glass, getting everyone's attention. I escort Joy back to our seats, not oblivious to the smiles directed at us by my parents.

They've wanted me to date Joy for years.

"I'd like to start the speeches," Amelia's dad begins, and for the next twenty minutes or so, we listen to him speak, along with her brother, Archer, and her sister.

Then, it's our turn.

My dad isn't much of a public speaker, so he left this task up to us.

Which is totally fine.

Levi and I stand, and before we do anything, we pick up our shot glasses, clink them together, and slam the whiskey. As the audience laughs, we fist-bump each other and then get down to business.

"I'm Jace, the handsome one."

"And I'm Levi, the favorite."

"Where does that leave Wyatt?" I ask the audience, glancing at my baby brother, who's already laughing. "Well, he's the baby."

"He might also be the smartest of all of us," Levi says, "because, well, look at this beautiful woman that he talked into marrying him."

More laughter.

"I mean, he stalked her at first," I continue and gesture to Levi, "despite having a cop for a brother."

"I don't think that's fair," Levi says, shaking his head and putting on a great show. "Technically, he just had a crush on his neighbor."

"Well, I'm grateful that it turned out to be mutual and that you didn't have to arrest him."

"Fair enough," Levi says with a nod. "In all seriousness, I would like to say thank you, Amelia. Thank you for loving our brother and for reminding him how to trust."

"Welcome to the Crawford family, sweetheart."

There are applause and hugs, and then, much to our surprise, Will Montgomery stands and asks for the mic.

"Hi, everyone. I haven't met all of Wyatt's family yet, so I'll introduce myself. I'm Will Montgomery, and I'm Lia's cousin. I just have a couple things to say.

"I had a feeling about you two from the beginning."

He winks at Lia, making her blush, and Wyatt busts up laughing. I make a mental note to ask him later what the inside joke is.

I glance over at Joy, who's hanging on Will's every word.

I'll get her naked later and remind her who, exactly, she has a crush on.

"I know the journey you've taken to get to this moment, Lia, and I just want to say, on behalf of my whole family, how very proud of you we are. You're strong, successful, smart, and you manage to do all of that *and* be a kind woman, despite what you've been through. You deserve this happiness, today and every day. You've come a long way, baby."

He lifts his glass, and we all follow suit.

"To Amelia and Wyatt."

"To Amelia and Wyatt!"

Joy sighs just before she takes a sip of her champagne.

"What's wrong?" I ask.

"Oh, nothing."

"I'm sitting *right here*," I remind her.

"I'm sorry, but it's *Will Montgomery*."

I take a sip of my drink, watching her over the rim. Finally, I lean in and whisper in her ear, "In about two hours, I'm going to strip you naked and fuck you so hard you won't remember your own name, let alone Will Montgomery's. You'll be screaming and begging for more."

"If this is the response I get from a harmless crush, I'll do it more often."

"What are you two whispering about over there?" Mom asks from across the table. She's happy today, with a perma-smile on her pretty face. "You should share with the table."

"This isn't your classroom," I remind her. "And I'm not a fourth-grader."

"Jace was just telling me that you might actually retire this year, Melody," Joy says with a smile and lays her hand on my thigh. She gives it a squeeze, and I'm grateful that the table's there to hide my hard-on.

"This is the year," Mom says with a nod. "It's time. Thirty years as a teacher is plenty."

"You'll be missed," Joy replies.

"But I'll be happy to have her home with me," Dad says, pulling Mom in to kiss her cheek. "It's time to start traveling and enjoying our nest egg."

"I couldn't agree more," Joy says with a smile. "Enjoy each other. That's what it's all about."

"How is your practice going, dear?" Mom asks Joy.

"It's great. I brought in two more doctors last year because I just couldn't keep up with it by myself anymore."

"Her office is awesome," I add, proud of the woman next to me. "She remodeled the place, and it's gorgeous. Also, she makes fresh cookies in the lobby for the clients."

"I need to get myself a dog," Levi says with a wink.

"The cookies make the place smell better," she insists. "And, sometimes, a girl needs a chocolate chip cookie."

"Makes sense to me," Mom says. "And I just want to say, it's nice to see you two together. Levi tells me you've been spending quite a bit of time together."

"We've been friends for years," I remind her softly, but Mom just shrugs a shoulder.

"I'm not getting any younger," she says. "Would it kill you

to marry this girl and make me happy?"

Joy spits out her champagne, and I just hide my face in my hand.

My mom doesn't have an issue with saying what's on her mind.

I never had a problem with that until today.

I glance over at Levi, who's laughing and eating his prime rib, happy to be out of the line of fire.

"Are you dating anyone?" I ask him.

"Nope." His grin is smug.

"Let's work on that and get them off my back."

"No way, this is way too much fun."

eight

Joy

"I forgot to tell you," I say the next morning as we're cozied up in Jace's bed, drinking coffee and enjoying a lazy start to the day, "Meredith Williams invited you, me, and Levi to her house this afternoon for a BBQ. I said yes. It sounds fun."

"Okay," Jace says, reading an article on his iPad.

"Whatcha reading?"

"An article on bloodless open-heart surgery in infants," he replies as calmly as if he'd said, *"I'm taking a quiz on my personality type based on my favorite color."*

"What are *you* reading?"

"I'm looking at Amelia's Instagram," I inform him. "She already put up a couple of photos from yesterday. Did you know she has like two million followers on here?"

"Yeah," he says and takes a sip of his coffee. "It's pretty cool."

"Her feed is beautiful," I say and smile at a photo of her and Wyatt as the pastor said, *"you may now kiss the bride."*

"I have to admit, I'm surprised your brother got married

again. I'm happy for him."

"Mm-hmm," Jace says, still reading his article.

"I mean, his ex was a grade-A bitch from Hell. I never did like her. And after everything that happened with catching her fucking that guy, and the way she acted all through the divorce, I wouldn't blame Wyatt if he swore off marriage forever."

"He did," Jace reminds me, "until he met Lia."

"Exactly." I sip from my mug and set my phone aside. "I like her. She seems sweet."

I glance over and find that Jace is still reading his article, and I'm beginning to feel ignored.

So I lie back on the bed and pull the covers down to my waist, exposing my naked breasts. My nipples pucker from the cool air.

I raise my arms over my head, thrusting my chest into the air a few more inches and sigh dramatically.

"What should we do before we go to the BBQ?" I ask, hoping he looks down at me and does *me*.

"Whatever you want," he says, his eyes still glued to his iPad.

I want you to fuck me seven ways to Sunday.

But rather than say that, I decide to be a little more . . . subtle. I drag one hand down my face, my neck, over my breast and belly, diving under the covers and finding my already hard clit.

I close my eyes and imagine that it's Jace's fingers tickling the nub, sending zings over my skin. I sigh, dip my fingertips into my wet pussy, then return to my clit, making slow, smooth movements back and forth. My hips move as if I were riding him.

Suddenly, Jace latches his lips around my nipple, and I open my eyes, smiling at him.

"Well, you *are* paying attention."

"I never stop paying attention to you," he says before kissing his way over to the other breast and sucking it hard into his mouth, then pulling up with a loud *pop*. "I heard every word you said. And I'll never complain about this kind of a show coming from you. It's fucking hot as hell. Do it every day if you want."

"It's your turn now," I say, pulling my hand away, but he shakes his head.

"No, I like watching you pleasure yourself." He tugs my nipple through his teeth, making me gasp, then goes back to kissing and sucking the underside of my breast, which is, coincidentally, more sensitive than the nipple itself. "I fucking love your nipples."

"They're too small."

"Not from this view," he says and rubs his nose back and forth over it. "Keep touching your clit. I want you to make yourself come."

My cheeks flush, and I'm suddenly shy. This was a *bad* idea. I just wanted to catch Jace's attention and let him take it from there.

The plan backfired on me.

He peels the covers off me and holds my thighs open as he watches my fingers move over the most sensitive part of myself.

"You're too nervous," he says and leans in to kiss my thigh, right next to my pussy. "Close your eyes and imagine that it's me. Just do what you'd want me to do."

That's easy. That's what I was doing to begin with. So, I follow his instructions and close my eyes. Now that I'm not watching him watch me, it's easier. My muscles loosen, and my thighs fall apart effortlessly.

"Gorgeous," he whispers before planting a wet kiss on my belly. "Put a finger inside."

I comply, but it's not enough. It's not *Jace*, so I add another finger and sigh, biting my lip.

"You like that?"

I nod, but he bites my side, hard. It makes my pussy squeeze around my fingers. "Words, Joy."

"I like it." My voice is breathy and needy. I'm chasing a killer orgasm.

"What do you need?"

"You."

I feel him smile against my skin, and it ticks my arousal up a notch, approaching unbearable.

"Jace."

"Yes, sweetheart."

"Please fuck me."

"Well, since you asked nicely." He flips me over, pulls my hips back and I hear him fumble with the condom. He pushes inside me, making me immediately explode with an orgasm. "Fucking hell." He grips onto my hair at the nape of my neck. He doesn't pull hard, but he has a firm hold, and it's maybe the best sex I've ever had in my life.

Although, I think that every time Jace and I have sex.

He clenches onto my hip with his free hand, and I bury my face in the pillows as he fucks me ruthlessly.

He groans and slows, pushing all the way to the root, and loses himself in me.

"Is that what you were after?" he asks in my ear, panting.

"Oh, yeah." I swallow hard, trying to catch my breath. "Yeah, that's the stuff."

He chuckles as he pulls out and collapses to the side of me. "So glad you approve."

"So glad you don't suck in bed," I reply and then laugh at his look of surprise. "What? I mean, it would not be good if you were a horrible lover."

"Are you saying you're just with me because of the way I bone you?"

"No." I shove my hair out of my face and laugh again. "Also, I love how romantic we are when we talk about having sex together."

"I can't believe you're just with me for the humping," he says, making me laugh harder. "Here I thought it was my sparkling wit and sense of humor."

"I'm all about bumping uglies," I say, still giggling. He cracks up, his abs clenching with the action, and I reach out to trace them with my fingertips. "These help, too."

"My stomach?"

"Your abs. They're hot. Let's keep them."

"I'll do my best."

"IT DIDN'T OCCUR to me that Will Montgomery would be here," I whisper to Jace as we carry our drinks out the back door to the gorgeous outdoor living space. Meredith, and her husband Mark have a beautiful home. It's something out of a Magnolia Home magazine.

I wouldn't be surprised if Joanna Gaines decorated it herself.

"The Williams family is very close to the Montgomerys," Jace says as he sits in a love seat and motions for me to join him.

"I know, I guess I just didn't consider it."

"Do you want to leave?"

I stare at him, blinking slowly. "No. No, I don't."

He smirks and sips his beer just as Levi joins us. Kids run around the yard and to the playhouse that's a replica of the main dwelling.

"This is a great house," I say, sipping my margarita. "Mer said Mark built it."

"He's a contractor," Levi says with a nod. "He and Isaac Montgomery run Montgomery Construction."

"Cool. There's a lot of people in this family."

"You're not kidding," Meg, Will's wife says as she joins us. "It intimidated the hell out of me when I was first with Will. But they're nice, and they only bite if you ask nicely."

I smirk and glance at Jace, remembering the way he sank his teeth into my side earlier. If I'm lucky, I'll have marks from it later.

Another woman comes outside and sits in the shade of the gazebo. My mouth is suddenly dry, and I can't remember my own name.

Because, holy shit, that's *Starla*.

As in, Starla the megastar. The voice of a generation. She can *sing*, dance, act. You name it, she can do it.

"Hey, girl," Starla says to Meg, then plops down in a chair and sighs. Her hair used to be bleach-blond and short, but it's grown long and is auburn now. She's a tiny, petite woman, yet a powerhouse all at the same time.

I saw her Belladonna tour several years ago, and I've had a massive girl crush on her ever since.

I had no idea that she'd be here today.

"Starla, this is Jace and Levi Crawford, Wyatt's brothers, and Joy Thompson."

"Hi," Starla says with a kind smile.

"Pleasure," Jace says as if he's meeting *anyone*, and Levi just nods.

I can't even remember how to say words, so I just smile.

"So, what do you do, Starla?" Levi asks, pulling me out of my speechlessness. I stare, wide-eyed at Jace, but he doesn't seem to know who she is either.

They're idiots. Have I taught them nothing?

I've failed them.

"I'm a musician," Starla says with a smile, tilting her head and hooking a piece of her hair behind her ear. Meg and I glance at each other.

"So, do you play the piano?" Jace asks.

I want to go hide in the playhouse. I can't *believe* them.

"I do," she says. "I play the guitar, too."

"That's awesome," Levi says. "But what do you do to pay the bills?"

"Are you kidding me?" I ask at last, staring at both of them with disgust, then turning to Starla. "I apologize for them. They don't get out much."

"No, it's actually really fun," Starla says with a laugh and turns back to the guys. "The music gig pays the bills."

"That's fantastic," Levi replies with a nod.

"What do you do?" Starla asks him.

"I'm a detective," he says.

"Oh, do you work with Matt?" she asks.

"Yes, in a different department, but also for the Seattle PD."

"Small world," she says.

"Do you really not know who she is?" I ask Jace, who glances at me and gives me a wide-eyed look that says he's lost.

I sigh, pull up my phone and find Starla on Wiki, then send him the link. He nods when he pulls it up on his phone, and then smiles down at me.

"Hi, guys," Meredith says as she joins us. "I'm so glad y'all came. There's food inside, but Will is already loading a plate so there may be none left by the time you get in there. I, however, am not eating much."

"Why?" I ask her.

"Because we have a show tonight and it always makes me nervous." She smiles and glances at Starla, who nods her head. "You guys have to come! Starla's playing in town, and Jax and I get to dance with her, just like the good ol' days."

"I'm in," I say immediately. Jace and Levi nod, not that I would have let them say no. We've just been invited to a Starla show. "And now I think I could use some food."

I jump up, hurrying inside, hopeful that Will is still by the food. Of course, he's married, and I'm in a relationship, and I'm just silly.

But holy fuck, he's hot.

And when I move into the dining room where the food is set up buffet-style, I come to a screeching halt.

Will is holding a sleeping baby girl against his shoulder as he dishes up a plate. For a mere mortal, it would be difficult, but this is Will Montgomery we're talking about. He's balancing the baby and dishing up his plate effortlessly. And when he turns his head to kiss the baby's cheek, I'm pretty sure my ovaries explode.

Damn. What is it about a man holding a sleeping baby?

"Hi, Joy," Jules says when she sees me. "Come on, we have tons of food. I hope you're hungry."

"I am definitely hungry," I agree. "And that baby is beautiful."

"Thanks," Will says with a proud smile. "I made this. Her name is Erin."

"Yes, he made her all alone," Natalie says, rolling her eyes.

"Nah, Meg helped." Will kisses the baby's head again. "Do you have kids, Joy?"

"No." I shake my head as I set a pulled pork slider on my plate. "I have a busy veterinary clinic, and I'm not sure I have time for kids."

"You can be successful and have kids," Jules says. "It's work, but it's possible."

"Well, I'm not in that position right now. But you never know."

"You never know," Jace says from behind me, startling me. I spin and find him smiling, not irritated in the least. "That looks good."

I take a bite of the slider. "Delicious."

"Wasn't talking about the food."

I blush, aware that we're not alone, and I don't know the Montgomery family well. But Will laughs as he walks past Jace.

"Good one, dude. You're going to fit in just fine."

"SO, SHE WAS engaged," I inform Jace after the show as we watch Starla take photos and sign autographs during her post-show meet and greet. We're with Meredith and Jax, Jules and Nat, and most of the Montgomery clan as we wait for Starla to finish up and celebrate with us.

"*Was?*" Jace asks.

"Yeah. His name was Rick. He was a race car driver and died in an accident just a few months before their wedding date. It was really sad."

"That's horrible," Jace says. Levi stands a few feet away, watching Starla and her fans closely.

"What the fuck is her security doing?" he demands. "Do they always let people touch her like that?"

"She doesn't seem upset," I say, watching as she says goodbye to the last person, takes a deep breath, and then walks over to us with a tired smile.

"That was fucking epic," she says, offering her fist to the others for a fist-bump. "Seattle always rocks the house. And having Mer and Jax with me again was just . . . amazing."

"It was wonderful and humbling," Meredith says with a laugh. "I'm reminded that I had two babies and haven't toured in about five years."

"You kicked ass," Starla assures her.

Jace and I are good at being wallflowers. We like to people watch, always have. We drink, stand together, and take everything in, then talk about it all after the event is over.

The good thing about tonight? It's loud enough that we can talk about it in real-time.

"Your brother has the hots for Starla."

Jace frowns. "How can you tell?"

"Seriously? Look at him. He's been watching her like she's the president and he's the secret service all night."

"The secret service doesn't watch the president," Jace says, shaking his head. "They watch everything *but* the president, in case they have to jump into action."

"Okay, he's been watching her like she's a chocolate cupcake and he wants dessert *real bad.*"

Jace snickers. "He does enjoy a chocolate cupcake."

We watch in avid fascination as Levi approaches Starla, and they step to the side so they can speak privately.

"I wonder what he's saying," Jace says.

"Let's do the lip-sync game," I suggest and take another sip of my martini. "Oh, Levi, you're so big and strong. I love that leather jacket you're wearing."

"Yes," Jace says, playing along, "my jacket is impressive. But you should see what I have going on under it."

"Really? Do you have muscles? Tattoos? Are you packing heat?"

"I do get very hot in the summertime, wearing this jacket."

I spit my drink out in laughter, then nudge Jace with my hip. "Maybe you should take your jacket off."

"No, I need to keep it on, to look mysterious. You sure are pretty. When are you going to sing?"

"Aww, you're making him sound stupid," I protest, frowning up at Jace. "We already heard her sing."

"He *is* stupid," Jace says with a laugh. "Okay, she's talking now. You go."

"I think we should go back to my place. I'll play my favorite playlist for you."

"Is that all you want to do?" Jace asks. "We could take a shower, and I could show you the size of my gun."

I giggle and then gasp. "Wait. Holy shit, they just traded phones. Your brother just snagged Starla's number."

"Atta boy," Jace murmurs.

"Levi has game," I say, impressed.

"I taught him everything he knows," Jace says, puffing out his chest, and I dissolve into laughter.

"You're so full of shit." I shake my head and take a sip of my drink. "You don't even know how to spell game."

"I'm hurt." He covers his heart with his hand. "Truly devastated."

"There, there." I pat him on the cheek, putting some force behind it. "I'll make it up to you later."

"I don't know, you're in a rough kind of mood."

"I'll be gentle with you."

He sweeps me up into his arms and kisses me soundly, then plants his lips next to my ear in that way he does when he has something just for me to hear.

"I'm *not* going to be gentle with you."

"Thank the baby Jesus."

nine

Joy

"**R**oom two needs her temperature taken again, please," I say to Susan, one of four techs on the staff today. "And three needs some immunizations drawn. I made a note in her chart."

"Done," she says with a smile. "You have a visitor in your office. He's hot and he brought lunch."

I sigh and throw my latex gloves into the trash. "I don't really have time today."

"Take twenty. I'll draw up the meds and take the temp. Dr. Myracle is caught up on his patients, so we're not behind today."

"Well, that *is* a miracle," I reply with a wink, wash my hands, and hurry into my office.

Jace is sitting at my desk, eating a burger from Red Mill. "Hungry?"

"So hungry, and I have seventeen minutes." I root around in the bag and retrieve my burger and fries, digging in immediately. "Mell me mm happnn."

Jace cocks a brow and chews his fries. "Come again?"

"Tell me what happened," I repeat after I swallow. "At your meeting."

He shrugs one shoulder. I can see by the tense lines in his face that it didn't go the way he wanted. Jace had his second meeting with the attorneys this morning.

"More of the same," he says. "They think they're closer to getting the family to settle out of court, and to say that I didn't do anything wrong."

"Do they want money? Is that what this is?"

He shoves a fry into his mouth. "Maybe. In their shoes, if I was convinced that the doctor caused the death of my father, I wouldn't settle. It wouldn't be about the money for me, it would be about proving that the doctor was in the wrong."

"Right. So, if they're willing to settle for a certain amount of money, which I'm assuming isn't peanuts, and say you did nothing wrong, it tells me they're just after the money."

"Exactly."

I sigh and chew on my burger. "I hate that."

"Me, too."

"I'm going to have to run for about ten miles after this burger," I say with a smile. "But damn, it tastes good."

"You work hard, you'll burn it off," he says and scowls. "I, on the other hand, need to step up my workout game since I'm not working. I don't want to lose these abs that you seem to enjoy."

"I'm not worried," I say, waving him off.

"You'll still love me with a dad bod?"

I laugh and toss my wrappers into the paper bag, then pull out a mirror to make sure I don't have anything stuck in my teeth before I stand. "You won't have a dad bod. If we're going to your house tonight, do you mind picking up Carl from my place? I don't want him to be alone all night."

"I can do that," he says with a smile. "I already got a litter box for him."

"You did?" He smiles, making my stomach clench. "You're so good to me."

I lean in to quickly kiss him, but he yanks me into his lap and kisses the fuck out of me.

"I have to remember how to be a doctor," I remind him when he comes up for air. "And I can't do that when you kiss me that way."

"I'm not sorry," he says with a satisfied grin as I maneuver my way out of his lap. "Have a good day, dear."

"See you later."

I hate keeping my patients waiting, even if it was just sixteen minutes. I do feel better after eating something, though.

"How is Daisy?" I ask as I walk into room two. Daisy, a Great Dane weighing in at almost two hundred pounds, hurries over to say hello to me.

"I think she might have eaten socks. Again," her owner, Alec, says with a sigh. "And she obliterated my carpet and subfloor the other day."

"Did you leave her alone all day again?" I ask as I feel around on her abdomen.

"I have to work," he insists, "so I can pay for all the damage she's doing to my house."

"She needs chew toys that are safe for her," I remind him and frown. "Yeah, there's something here."

"Shit," he mutters, rubbing his forehead. "Another surgery?"

"Let me do an X-ray to see how big it is, but if it might

obstruct her intestines, yes, she'll need surgery again."

"Fuck," he whispers. "I don't know if I can keep her."

"I warned you when you adopted her that she would grow to be the size of a small horse and that she would be difficult for the first few years until she mellowed out."

"I know."

"And you didn't believe me."

"I thought the kids would help with her more," he admits. He'd divorced from his wife, and as an apology, he bought his kids a dog. "Not sure why, considering they only see me on the weekends."

"Maybe Daisy could go back and forth with the kids?" I suggest, but he shakes his head.

"My ex is allergic," he says. "She's already pissed that the kids come home with dog hair on their stuff."

"If you decide to rehome her, please don't surrender her to the animal shelter," I plead with him. "The odds of her being adopted there are slim, due to her size."

"I'll let you know first," he says with a nod. "But let's find out what the damages are today."

"Okay, I'm going to take her back for an X-ray real quick, and then I'll bring her back to you."

He nods, and I take Daisy's leash, leading her through the back door of the exam room to our work area. This is where we do X-rays, blood draws, and kennel the patients that have to stay with us longer than a few hours.

"Daisy needs an abdominal X-ray," I inform Susan. "Can you help me with this real quick?"

"Sure," she says, setting aside what she was doing and walking with me to the X-ray machine. As usual, she talks while we work. "I have a question."

"Shoot."

"Why do we have to change the way we store the surgical instruments?"

I frown at her over Daisy's back as I adjust the camera on the dog's belly.

"We don't."

"According to Dr. Crawford, we do."

I blink, confused. "Did he tell you that?"

She nods as we take the photo and then adjust Daisy and the machine for another view. "He was looking at the instruments and told us to switch it up because it would be more convenient for you and the other doctors during surgery. I'm sorry if the way we've been doing it has been a problem for you during procedures."

I take a deep breath and then blow it out, trying to keep my temper at bay. "You don't need to change anything. I like it exactly the way it is. Hell, I *trained* you all to do it that way because it's the way I prefer it."

She nods, clearly not happy that Jace made himself at home in my clinic, and I agree with her.

Once Daisy is finished with the X-ray, I turn to Susan. "Will you please take her back into room two. I'll be there in just a few moments to go over the X-ray with Alec. I'm going to have a quick chat with Jace."

"You bet," she says, leading a happy Daisy away from me.

I go in search of Jace and find him in my operating room, looking under the sink.

"It's really clean under here," he says without looking at me. "I'm impressed."

"Surgery requires cleanliness," I remind him, and he glances up in surprise.

"I thought you were Susan."

"No." I prop my hands on my hips. "What are you doing, Jace?"

"Just looking around," he says casually. "I didn't think you'd mind."

"Well, I do." His head whips up in surprise. "Jace, you're not a vet. I need my surgical instruments the way they are for the kind of surgery *I* do. This is my clinic, not Seattle General."

"Hey, I was just—"

"I know," I interrupt. "But I need you to go, please. I'll see you tonight."

He holds up his hands, clearly hurt, and marches away, through the door and out of the clinic without a word.

I feel bad for about three seconds. He *was* just trying to help. But he can't just come in here and take over. This is my business. This is my staff.

So, I hurry back to give Alec the bad news of another surgery to remove socks from his dog's abdomen, determined to worry about Jace later.

I'M BONE-TIRED. IT'S three hours past the normal end to my day. I had to perform surgery on poor Daisy, and had two more emergencies come in.

I'm on call tonight, and I'm praying that no one has any needs overnight. I could use a good night's sleep.

First, though, I need to make up with my boyfriend. Because

even though I wasn't in the wrong, I did hurt his feelings, and I hate that with every fiber of my being.

I pull into Jace's driveway and walk through his door, carrying two cobb salads from our favorite place. I figured we could both use something healthy after our burgers and fries for lunch.

"Hello?" I call out, but I don't see Jace. The lights are on in his kitchen and living room, so I set the salads on the island and walk back to the bedroom, hoping to find him there.

And boy, do I find him.

He's doing pull-ups on a contraption that he's attached to his doorframe, easily moving up and down in smooth motions. His feet are tucked up so they don't brush the floor.

He's topless.

And I'm immediately turned on to a level ten.

"Well, hello there," I say, crossing my arms and watching as he finishes three more, then he stands, breathing hard. There's a thin sheen of sweat on his olive skin.

I want to lick him.

"Hey," he says. He doesn't exactly seem ecstatic to see me.

"I brought dinner."

"I ate," he says. "After you texted and said you'd be late."

"Okay, your salad will keep."

He nods and moves into push-ups. I'm silent and enjoy the flex of his back and how his core engages as he pounds out twenty-five of them. The dimples above his ass show above the low-slung basketball shorts he's wearing.

Good lord, the man is sex on a cracker.

When he stands again and still doesn't talk to me, I rush to him and wrap my arms around his waist, holding on tightly because I just can't stand the *silence* from him. We don't do the silent treatment.

He doesn't hug me back, but he doesn't push me away either, so I take that as a win.

"I need you to talk to me," I murmur against his skin. "I don't even care that you're sweaty. I'm not moving until you talk to me."

He finally, *finally*, buries his lips in my hair and kisses my head, and my world is set to rights again.

"I'm going crazy," he admits quietly. "I know I have projects here, and things I *could* do, but I need to work, Joy."

"I know." I pull away and tip my head back so I can look at his face. I hate seeing the torture in his gorgeous grey eyes. "I'm so sorry this is happening."

"What if I can't operate anymore?"

I scowl. "What?"

"What if I've spent too much time away and I just can't do it?"

"That's not even an option," I reply immediately. "Jace, it's been two weeks. You are the leading cardiothoracic surgeon in the fucking *country*. You haven't forgotten it."

"It's not like riding a bike."

"And you don't have dementia," I remind him. "I understand that you're going stir-crazy. You went from working sixty-plus hours a week to none, and that has to be incredibly frustrating."

"You have no idea." He pulls out of my arms and walks to the windows that look out over Seattle. It's dark now, and the city is lit up. I can see Jace's reflection in the glass. "I'm sorry," he says before spinning around to look me in the face. "I'm sorry for intruding on your business today."

"Jace, it wasn't that big—"

"No, it was completely disrespectful and out of line," he says. "If you'd walked into my operating room and started rearranging things, I would have spanked your ass before throwing you out on it."

I bite my lip, trying to hide a smile.

"Can we still try the spanking thing?"

He blows out a breath with a chuckle and props his hands on his hips. "I'm trying to be serious here."

"I know." I hurry to him and hug him again. "Apology accepted. Thank you."

"You're welcome. How was your day?"

"It sucked." I sigh, my ear against his heart. I love the *thump thump thump*. "I had three emergency surgeries. That Great Dane you saw?"

"Yeah?"

"She ate four socks, and they were stuck in her small intestine."

"Ouch."

"She has behavioral issues, mostly because of the owner, who doesn't want to listen to me. And then I had a pug come in with a laceration to his eye, which he lost, four spay or neuters, and a dog I couldn't save from being hit by a car."

"Oh, baby," he says, rubbing his hands up and down my arms. "That's a rough day."

"I hate it when the animal dies," I admit. "It's just so sad. Did I tell you that I'm getting the additional licensing and building my own crematory behind the clinic? So I can cremate the animals there?"

"No." He kisses my forehead. "You didn't mention it."

"I just secured the loan for it," I reply. "I want to offer it to my clients."

"You need to eat and get some rest."

"I know. I'm on call tonight, and I'm praying that no one

needs me. I'm beat."

He takes my hand and leads me out to the kitchen. "Sit."

"Yes, sir." I grin as I prop myself in the stool at the island, watching as he plates my salad and brings it to me with a bottle of water. "Thank you. What did you eat?"

"Pizza."

"Jace!"

"I know." He cringes. "Why do you think I was doing all the exercising when you got here? I have to change this diet."

"This weekend, I'm going to do some meal prep," I announce. "So we're not tempted to keep eating out."

"I'll help," he says with a smile. "Can we have pizza?"

"No."

"Killjoy." He winks at me. He thinks he's funny.

I smirk and take a bite of my salad. "Salad is delicious."

"It's rabbit food."

"You're a *cardiologist*," I remind him. "You know better than anyone what bad food does to your heart."

"Well, then they shouldn't make it so delicious."

"You're a hot mess."

"But I'm hot," he says with a cocky grin that makes my lady parts come to life. "That's what you're saying."

"You're not bad," I concede.

"I saw the way you watched me doing those pull-ups," he says as he saunters around the island. "Admit it."

"I mean, you were half-naked, so . . ."

"Are you done with that salad?"

"Yeah."

"Good."

He lifts me onto the island and pulls my scrub pants down

my hips. I lift up so he can peel them, along with my panties, down my legs and toss them aside.

"The countertop is cold."

"I'm about to warm you up."

And good to his word, he spreads my legs and presses his lips to my core, sucking and licking and sending me over the moon faster than I knew was possible.

"Holy fuck!" I cry out as I lean back on my elbows and give in to an earth-shattering orgasm.

He kisses my thighs and, before I know it, he's inside me, his hands framing my face and his eyes on mine as he slowly pulls his hips back and then slams back inside.

"Is this makeup sex?" I ask.

"Yeah."

"I rather like it."

He sets a punishing rhythm, in and out, hard and fast until he comes, biting my shoulder.

"No more fighting," he growls against my neck. "I don't like it."

"But it leads to this, and this is pretty fantastic." I bury my fingers in his hair, brushing it softly.

"We can do this without the fighting." He kisses my cheek, and then my lips. I can still taste myself on him. "Okay?"

"Okay."

I know we'll have arguments from time to time. We're human, after all, but I agree that fighting isn't my thing. Some couples thrive on the bickering and the drama, but I don't.

And I'm relieved that he doesn't either.

He pulls out of me and swears.

"Um, Joy?"

"Yeah?"

"I forgot a condom." His face is sober. "I'm sorry, babe. I can't believe I did that."

"We should be fine," I reply as I hop off the counter and reach for my clothes. "It's not the right time of month for me to get pregnant."

"Are you sure?"

"Yeah." I pat his cheek and lean up to kiss his lips. "Don't worry."

"Okay."

"I'm going to take a shower and then probably go to bed. I'm beat."

"Do you mind if I read while you sleep?" he asks.

"Not at all."

I take a quick shower, not bothering to wash my hair, and when I walk into the bedroom, Jace is sitting on the bed, reading his iPad with Carl curled up next to him, purring like crazy.

"More bloodless surgeries?" I ask as I smooth lotion over my legs and then climb under the covers.

"No, this is on a quadruple bypass," he says, already absorbed in the article. His beautiful hands move as he reads as if he's performing the surgery himself.

He blows me away. As if he could forget how to perform surgery. It would never happen.

He's too incredibly talented.

I yawn and turn away from him so the light is to my back and check my phone to make sure the sound is on in case I get called.

I close my eyes and fall asleep.

ten

Jace

Joy's phone is ringing.

She reaches for it, and I check the time. 2:49 in the morning. She only got about four hours of sleep.

I, however, got less than two. Not that it matters. I'm used to living on very little rest.

"Are they on their way to the clinic?" she asks as she hurries from the bed, reaching for a clean pair of scrubs. "I'll be there in twenty. Get the IV going, and the anesthesia, just in case. It sounds like she may need a C-section."

Joy ends the call and tosses the phone onto the bed.

"I have to go in."

"I'm driving," I say, already stepping into my shorts and reaching for a T-shirt.

"You don't have to go. You should get some sleep."

"I'm awake, and I'd like to come along."

She smiles as she steps into her shoes and nods. "Let's go, then."

The drive to the clinic is roughly fifteen minutes. When we arrive, Joy jumps out of my car, barely taking the time to slam her door shut before she runs into the building. I'm on her heels as she rushes into a surgery room where a beautiful German Shepherd is lying on an exam table, panting.

"She had one baby that I already gave to her," the owner says, wringing her hands with worry and gesturing to the tech. "But it's been several hours, and no more are coming."

Joy is gowned and gloved up and examining the dog, who's whimpering softly and looking up at Joy with scared, brown eyes.

"That's it, darling girl," Joy croons to the canine. "These little ones are stuck, aren't they?"

She frowns up at the owner. "*This* is what happens when you let a dog get pregnant too young. She's not even a year old. Her body isn't developed enough to give birth."

Joy's all business. All doctor. I'm standing at the edge of the room, watching her every move, so caught up in all of it that I can't move.

"We need to do a C-section, Charity," she says to her night-time tech.

"Is that necessary?" the owner asks. "I mean, it'll be so expensive."

"Get her out of here," she says to Charity, who immediately escorts the owner out of the surgery room to the waiting room, where I can hear Bill telling her to fuck off.

Seems appropriate.

"I know, angel. It hurts." She pets the dog gently with one hand while the other continues to examine the business end. "We're going to let you take a nap while these babies are born. You rest now."

"Do you need me?" I ask Joy, and she glances up at me as if she forgot I was here. "I'm an extra pair of hands. I'll do whatever you want."

"Actually, I might need you," she says with a nod. "Go ahead and wash your hands and suit and glove up. I may need you to hold puppies."

"Jesus, that lady is a piece of work," Charity says when she hurries back into the room. "I told her to stay there until one of us comes to get her."

"Thank you," Joy says as she reaches for an IV. "We need to put her under and get these puppies out. They're stuck in the birth canal. They're just too big for her. She's too young for this."

"Pisses me off when people don't listen," Charity murmurs.

"Story of our lives," Joy replies with a sigh. I scrub, pull on gloves and a surgical gown, and walk toward Joy, but stay back, just waiting to help if she needs me.

I've never watched her in action before. I *knew* she was an animal doctor, and that she's an excellent one, but I've never seen her perform surgery.

She is sexy as fuck wielding a scalpel, already elbow-deep in the abdomen of the dog.

"Here's puppy two," she says since the first puppy was born naturally. Charity takes it, wraps it in a towel and begins to rub it vigorously. "She's keeping it warm," Joy informs me. "Feels like there are four still in here."

"Six puppies?"

"That's pretty small for a German Shepherd litter," she says as she pulls out another puppy, passing it to Charity again.

"Here's a towel," Charity says. "They'll start coming fast now."

She's not wrong. In less than two minutes, the rest of the puppies are born, and we go to work wrapping them, rubbing them to keep them warm, and making sure they're breathing.

Which, thankfully, all of them are.

We've cleaned them up, and they're huddled together under a heating lamp while Joy takes care of the mama.

"Her uterus is destroyed," Joy mumbles as she reaches for a sponge to clean up some of the blood. "Charity, I have to do a hysterectomy."

"That'll piss the owner off," Charity says. "She wanted her as a breeding dog."

"Idiot," Joy mutters. "Jace, pass me that clamp."

I do as I'm told, on this side of a surgery for the first time since my residency, and I'm in awe of Joy and the work she's doing on this animal.

"You know, if this vet thing doesn't work out, you could be an OB/GYN," I suggest with a smile.

"I don't deliver human babies," she replies with a grin. "Sutures, please."

I comply and watch as she sews the dog internally before closing her up and suturing the wound.

"Charity, who comes on when you're done at six?"

"Leslie," Charity replies as she feeds one of the puppies from the tiniest bottle I've ever seen.

"Good. This mama needs to stay here with her babies for at least three days. I want to watch this incision. You can bring the owner back in."

"How is she?" the owner asks as she walks in. "How many puppies are there?"

"Six," Joy says as she wipes her hands on a towel. "All healthy. Their mama had some complications, and I had to perform a hysterectomy."

"What?" The woman stares at Joy in horror. "How *dare* you? She's a source of income for me."

"Not anymore," Joy replies, tossing her towel into a hamper. "Because you bred her so young, her uterus was destroyed, and any further litters could have killed her."

"Damn it," the other woman mutters, shaking her head. "Well, I guess selling these puppies will help pay for what I have invested in her. I might break even."

"I need to keep all of them here for three days while Mom recovers."

"More vet bills," the owner says, rubbing her eyes. I can see Joy getting more and more angry by the moment.

"You know, she could have died," Joy reminds the woman. "What you did here was very irresponsible."

"I don't need a lecture from you," the lady snarls. "I make a living the best I can, just like you do. I'll sell her and the puppies, and then I'll have to start over."

"How about this?" Joy says, crossing her arms over her chest, "I'll write off your entire bill *and* keep the dog and the puppies. You can walk out of here and wash your hands of the whole thing."

"Those pups were going to be a thousand dollars a piece," the woman replies with a frown.

"My bill for tonight and the next three days while she's here is roughly seven thousand," Joy says without skipping a beat. "I think what I'm offering is more than fair."

The woman bites her lip and looks at the dog for about three seconds, then shrugs. "Fine."

"One more condition," Joy says. "In the future, I won't care for any of your animals. I don't work with unethical clients."

"Whatever." The woman rolls her eyes and stomps out without even looking at the sweet puppies sleeping under the light or the mama on the table.

"So now we have a dog and six puppies," Joy says with a sigh. "Jesus, what did I just do?"

"You saved their lives," I reply softly, running my fingers down her cheek.

"He's right," Charity says. "When she arrived, she said the dog doesn't even have a name. She didn't care enough to *name* her."

Joy blows out a breath and leans in to kiss the dog's cheek. "You're waking up," she murmurs. "You're a mama now, sweet girl. And they're all safe and healthy. We'll let you feed them tomorrow, but in the meantime, my friends are helping you out."

"Nothing sweeter than a baby," Charity says, feeding yet another puppy.

"You're mine now," Joy says to the dog, surprising me. I thought for sure she'd find her a forever home. "And your name is Angela."

The dog whimpers groggily, and Joy kisses her again then reaches for a pup. One by one, she shows the dog her babies, lets her sniff and lick them, then tucks them away.

"We'll put them with her around noon. In the meantime, let's keep them under the lamp and feed them every hour. I'll call Mindi in to be on puppy duty for the morning."

"I can stay, too," Charity offers, but Joy shakes her head.

"No, you need some rest. Do you want me to stay with you until Leslie arrives at six?"

"Nah, it's not long," Charity says. "Angela will sleep, and I get to snuggle brand new puppies. It's really a tough gig."

Joy smiles and rubs her face. "I think I'll go try to rest. I'm off today, but I'll call and check in later this morning."

"Okay," Charity replies, waving us off as we walk back out to my car. We're quiet on the drive home, and when I pull into the garage, I glance over to find that she's asleep.

I walk around the car, open her door, and lift her into my arms, carrying her inside. She wakes up and wraps her arms around my neck, burying her face near my shoulder.

"I'm taking you to bed," I inform her.

"I can't have sex right now," she says, kissing my shirt. "I'm too tired."

"No sex for you. Although watching you work might be the sexiest fucking thing I've ever seen."

Her eyes spring open, and she stares at me as I set her on her feet by the bed.

"Seriously?"

"Oh, yeah." I swallow hard, willing my dick to calm the fuck down. "You're *amazing*, Joy. Your skill, your professionalism. Jesus, it was . . . fascinating."

"It was just a C-section. You should see me reconstruct a knee."

"I'm serious." I pace the room as Joy sits on the edge of the bed, watching me. "I've always known that you're excellent at your job, but witnessing it is something else altogether."

"Thank you," she murmurs, a smile tickling her lips. "That means a lot, Jace."

"I'm proud of you." The words are pouring out of me now. I walk back to her, pulling her into my arms. I can't stop touching her.

I don't ever want to stop touching her.

"I've loved you for almost half my life," I say into her hair. "But Joy, I'm *in* love with you."

She stills in my arms, and I simply wait. My Joy is a thinker, and sometimes, she needs to process things.

But when I hear a sniffle, I pull back to look into her tear-soaked eyes.

"Joy?"

"I'm in love with you, too," she whispers and looks away from me. She fiddles with the necklace she wears and stares at my neck.

"Look at me."

Her eyes move to mine again.

"Why does it make you sad?" I ask tenderly while wiping a tear away with my thumb.

"I'm not sad," she says and sniffs, making me smile. "I'm surprised. And I have a confession."

"Seems this is the time for them." I brush another tear, then lift her again and sit in the chair in the corner of my bedroom with Joy in my lap. She's a petite woman and fits perfectly against me, whether we're having sex or just sitting like this.

"I've been in love with you for a long time."

I stare at her in surprise, then frown. "Why didn't you ever say anything?"

She cocks a brow and gives me the don't-be-dumb look.

"Because we're in the *friend* zone."

"Were," I correct her.

"Right. We were in the friend zone. And I didn't want to screw it up because you're my best friend."

"Likewise," I say with a sigh. "But we're not screwing it up, Joy. It's way better, and I didn't think it *could* get better."

"I know," she whispers, burying her face in my neck. She's exhausted, and I should put her to bed, but I'm selfish. Having her in my arms is heaven. "I love you, Dr. Crawford."

She yawns, and I smile, my heart beating double-time. "I love you too, Dr. Thompson."

"WE NEED THE following," Joy says as we walk into the grocery store. I reach for a small cart, but she shakes her head and points to the big one.

Apparently, we're buying out the store.

"Salad stuff, including kale, chicken breasts, Brussels sprouts, squash, a case of water, non-fat milk, yogurt, eggs, mushrooms, ground beef, and anything else I see that I have to have."

"That list is all over the place," I inform her. "Don't you write your list by category? Like, all the dairy together, all the produce, and so on?"

She shrugs a shoulder as she leads me to the produce section. "I wrote this a little at a time, so I jotted things as they came to me." She reaches for a bag of green beans. "Would you rather have green beans over the Brussels sprouts?"

"Either is fine. I'm going to go grab a couple of apples."

"Okay," she says, not even glancing my way as I walk to the display of fruit.

I prefer the Honeycrisp, grown here in Washington. I check for bruises and place them in a bag, then turn to fetch a couple of bananas.

"Hi."

I glance up to find a woman grinning at me. She has dark

hair, cut short. Her face is pretty, and she's curvy in all the right places. At another time in my life, I would have been interested.

"Hello."

"I've seen you in here a few times," she continues. "You must live nearby."

"Uh, not far, yeah."

She nods. "I'm Lisa."

"Hi, Lisa, I'm Joy." The woman I love is suddenly standing next to me, her hand in mine, and a bright, fake-as-fuck smile on her face aimed at Lisa. "How are you?"

"Oh, I'm fine." Lisa's smile falls. "Have a good day."

"You too, Lisa!" Joy waves at the other woman as she pushes her cart out of the produce section, then gives her retreating back the stink-eye.

"She was a friendly woman," I comment, knowing full well that Joy is irritated. I can't blame her. If some dude started flirting with her over the kumquats, I'd lay him out.

"You're not allowed to shop by yourself," she says, not looking me in the eyes as she bags a bunch of kale. "In fact, just leave the shopping to me."

"Joy, I was just kidding." I laugh when she tosses the kale into the cart harder than she needs to. I can tell she thinks it's funny too as she's trying to suppress a grin. "I wouldn't dare flirt with another woman when you're in the store."

She glares at me, and I laugh harder. I bury my fist in the hair at the back of her head and pull her to me for a long, deep kiss. I give zero shits that we're in the middle of the produce section.

"I only have eyes for you, babe."

She grins. "I know. But that was kind of fun."

"I wasn't squirming," I inform her.

"And I wasn't actually mad," she replies. "You're hot. Girls will flirt with you."

"And if you'd been five seconds later, you would have heard me tell her that I have a scorching-hot girlfriend."

"As it should be," she says with a nod, making me grin. "Now, we need the meat department."

"I'll show you the meat department," I murmur in her ear, making her giggle.

"You're ridiculous."

"You love me."

She shrugs a shoulder, then nods. "Okay, I do. I love you and your ridiculousness."

An hour later, I'm hauling groceries from the car to the kitchen. We got everything on Joy's list, along with about fifty things that *weren't* on her list.

"I thought the point of this was for us to eat cleaner," I say, pulling out a bag of Oreos from a grocery sack.

"I'll eat like three of those a day," she says with a frown.

"And I'll eat the rest of the bag in one sitting."

"Then I'll hide them from you." She bats her eyelashes at me and unboxes the disposable Tupperware containers she bought for the meal prep portion of this operation. "I'm going to make individual salads, so all we have to do is put dressing on them. I'm also going to grill up a bunch of chicken breasts, mushrooms, green beans, and so on. So there will be a complete meal in each container."

"Okay, Rachael Ray, let's do it."

For the rest of the afternoon, we chop, sauté, grill, and assemble our meals for the week. My house smells amazing.

"I don't think I've ever done this much cooking in this

kitchen," I say as we seal the tops on the last of the containers.

"This space is gorgeous," she says with a sigh. "It should be cooked in often."

"Well now that you're here, it will be."

She nods, but I can tell something's on her mind.

"What are you thinking?" I ask.

"I should probably check on my house," she says with a quirk of her lip.

"We can load this up, along with Carl, and stay at your place for a few days."

"You don't mind?"

"As long as I'm with you, I don't mind at all."

eleven

Joy

"Why am I going to this?" Noel asks me for the fifth time. Jace just dropped us off at a spot in Bellevue that's known for good food and even better music. "I don't know any of these girls."

"Because we need a girls' night out," I inform her again. "And you'll *like* these women. I promise. They're not bitches."

"Everyone's nice to you," she says as we walk down the sidewalk in our heels. "Because you're likeable."

"Well, so are you." We head into the bar. It's not quite hopping yet, and I spy our party right away at a big round booth in the back. "There they are."

"Joy!" Meredith exclaims and waves in excitement.

"Hi," I say with a smile and gesture to my sister. "This is Noel. Noel, this is Meredith Williams, and Amelia Crawford, who I believe you've met."

"Definitely," Noel says with a nod. "Hi, Lia."

"Hey, girl," Lia says. "This is my sister, Anastasia."

"We need name tags," Noel says as we scoot our way into the booth.

"Oh, honey, this is nothing," Meredith says with a laugh. "You should see my family. I've been part of it for over five years now, and there are days that I think we need to wear name tags."

"It's a huge family," Anastasia agrees with a nod. "But fun. And let's not forget, sexy as hell. I mean, the level of hotness that exists in that family should be illegal."

"I'll have a champagne with pomegranate," I inform the waitress, and Noel orders the same. We also place an order of just about everything on the appetizer menu. "How was your honeymoon, Lia?"

"The best," she says with a grin, sipping her martini. "Wyatt took me to Paris for fashion week."

"No," Noel says, her eyes wide in shock. "Stop it."

"It's true." Lia sighs. "VIP all the way, too. Front-row seats. It was off the fucking hook."

"Oh my God, that's awesome," Noel says, and I know that she and Lia will be good friends. They share a love of fashion and makeup and all things girly that I just don't have a passion for.

"I have some fun makeup ideas for the kids," Lia informs Meredith.

"Awesome," Mer says, clapping her hands. "Lia's been working with me and the kids in my studio and does all of the makeup for our recitals."

"They're cute," Lia says with a smile.

"And are you still going to keep up with your YouTube channel?" I ask her.

"Oh, yeah, I love it, and it's a great source of income," Lia says with a nod. "But what I really want to know is, what's up with you and Jace? Wyatt said you've always just been friends, but you were more than friendly at our wedding."

"I love gossip like this," Anastasia says, sipping her drink. "We need more nights out."

"Well, we've been friends since our freshman year of college," I reply with a smile and glance at Noel, who's also smiling. "But over the past couple of months, things have grown more . . . intense."

"So you're fucking," Mer says with a grin. "I love it. Keep talking, and use all the dirty words."

I laugh and reach for an onion ring. "The sex is . . . wow."

"I just need to add something," Noel says, holding up a hand. "As someone who's witnessed this from the beginning. The Jace you all know *now* is not the Jace from almost fifteen years ago."

"How so?" Anastasia asks.

"He was a little nerdy," I say, but Noel rolls her eyes.

"No, he was a *lot* nerdy. And shy. And just not confident at all."

"I mean, he was nineteen," I remind everyone and glare at my sister. "You're making him sound awful, and he was *not* awful. He was young."

"But man, did he grow up," Noel says with a smile.

"Sometimes, it takes a person a while to come into their own," Meredith says with a shrug. "I was the skinniest, scrawniest girl ever. Of course, dance kept me small, but I didn't blossom until after school."

"Jace's always been a great guy," I continue, "and we've stayed close all these years. He's an amazing doctor. I have a lot of respect for him."

"And his penis," Anastasia says with a wink, making us all giggle.

"It's evolved from friendship love to romantic love," I continue. "And the sex is off the hizzy."

"Atta girl," Lia says, reaching her hand out to bump mine. "I love Jace. He's the best. When I didn't know if things would work out between Wyatt and me, he was there to listen, and he never judged me."

"That's Jace," I agree with a nod. "He's a good friend."

"What about you, Noel?" Meredith asks. "Are you seeing anyone?"

"Who has time?" Noel asks with a gusty breath. "I work non-stop. So, unless he wants to pick out curtains or a sofa, I'm probably not going to meet him."

"Same," Anastasia says. "The only men I meet are grooms and new dads."

"Well, that one groom did come on to you," Lia says, and Anastasia rolls her eyes.

"Don't remind me. What a creep."

"Joy, has Levi said anything to you about Starla?" Meredith asks, and Noel stares at me in shock.

"*Starla?*" Noel screeches. "As in the pop star?"

"That's the one," I reply and fill her in on the concert and Levi leaving with her.

"You didn't tell me!"

"I'm sorry, it's been busy," I say with a shrug. "I haven't seen Levi much, but no, I don't think he's said anything."

"Starla won't talk about it either," Mer says, tapping her chin in thought. "I want to know if there's something ongoing there, or if it was just a one-night thing. Frankly, Starla hasn't given anyone the time of day since Rick died, and that was more than four years ago now."

"Wow," I breathe. "I had no idea. I remember his accident was all over the news. It was sad."

"It devastated her," Mer says. "So, when she left the venue with Levi, I was excited for her."

"Wait, let me get this straight," Noel says, shaking her head. "You're *friends* with Starla?"

"Oh, yeah, long-time friends. I used to tour with her as a backup dancer, but now I own a studio here in Seattle with my dance partner, Jax, and I'm a mom. I danced with Starla when she was in Seattle for old times' sake, but I hung up my touring shoes years ago."

"That's so awesome," Noel says.

"I'll ask Levi about it the next time I see him," I offer.

"So will I," Lia says with a wink. "We'll get the deets."

"You guys, it's the cha-cha slide," Meredith exclaims, shimmying her way out of the booth. "Come on!"

"I don't know how to do it," I say with a laugh.

"I'll show you, it's easy. Let's go."

"WHERE IS HE?" Noel asks as we stand on the sidewalk. Jace is on his way to pick us up, and rather than wait for him inside, we decided to get some fresh air. Noel is holding her heels in her hands.

"On his way. You're going to get flesh-eating bacteria or something, standing on the sidewalk in your bare feet."

"I let a stranger kiss me on the dance floor," she reminds me, and I break out in giggles. Gosh, she's funny when we've been drinking. "I don't think I need to worry about the sidewalk."

"Just don't call me when you have tetanus in your toes."

"That's disgusting," Noel says as Jace pulls up to the curb. He's in my car since his is just a two-seater.

"Hi, ladies," he says with a smile. Noel climbs into the back seat, and I fall into the passenger seat, smiling at him.

"You're hot," I inform him.

"And you're drunk," he says with a laugh. "I haven't seen you like this in years."

"I haven't done this in years," I reply with a frown. "I'm always the responsible one."

"We need more girls' nights out," Noel informs us from the back seat. "With champagne and celebrity gossip and kisses from strangers on the dance floor."

Jace's head whips to mine, and he scowls.

"It's hot when you're jealous," I inform him.

"You *kissed a stranger?*"

"Not her, you idiot. *Me,*" Noel says with a giggle. "She's too hung up on you to even dance with a boy."

Jace reaches over to take my hand in his and kisses the back of my knuckles. "Good girl."

"Oh, that sounded dominant," Noel says as she scoots forward. "Are you a dominant? Like, do you tie her up and use a flogger and have a red room of pain?"

"You read too many books," I say with a giggle. "But I wouldn't mind the flogger."

"Good God," Jace mutters, rubbing his fingers over his lips. "You girls shouldn't be out alone when you're this drunk. It's not safe."

"We're perfectly safe," I reply.

"Yeah, I carry mace," Noel says primly. "And don't change the subject. Do you use butt plugs?"

I blow a raspberry as I laugh my ass off, and Jace chuckles.

"Not yet," he says.

"I want to play with butt plugs," Noel says, almost pouting in the back seat. "I need to find a fuck buddy. I don't want anything permanent or serious because I don't have time for that, but sometimes, a girl just needs something shoved up her ass."

"Oh my God!" I exclaim, shocked and laughing harder than I have in years. "Noel, you do *not* want that."

"Okay, maybe not. But he should shove something somewhere."

"You're home," Jace says, sounding ridiculously relieved.

"Do you need me to help you inside?" I ask my sister, but she shakes her head as she climbs out of the car.

"Call you tomorrow," she says, waving without looking back as she stumbles up the walk to her small house. Once she's inside, Jace pulls away from the curb, and I make a dive for his pants.

"What are you doing?"

"Unzipping your pants," I reply as if that should be self-evident.

"Why?"

"This seatbelt is in my way." I unclip it and let it zoom away, giving me easier access to his perfect dick.

Once he's unzipped and I've pushed aside his clothes, I'm delighted to find that he's already hard.

"Did the butt plug talk do this to you?"

"No, you unzipping my pants did it," he says. "Joy, I can't drive like this."

"You're a smart man," I say and drag the tip of my tongue around the crown of his cock. "You can drive."

"Fuck me, Joy."

"I am." I lower over him, taking him to the back of my throat, and then pull up again as I lick him firmly. "Can't wait 'til we get home."

He buries one hand in my hair, and I go to work on him, licking the length of him along that rigid vein that sticks out when he's super turned on—the way he is now. He's breathing hard and moans every time I sink down and grip him with my lips, milking him with my mouth.

He tastes salty, and his skin is smooth.

"Delicious," I say when I come up for air. "I love your cock."

"Jesus Christ, if you keep this up, I'll come."

"Oh, good." I'm jacking him with my fist and paying a *lot* of attention to the tip, until finally I sink down once more and he comes in my mouth, spraying the back of my throat.

It doesn't trigger my gag reflex. Instead, it's possibly the sexiest thing that's ever happened when I'm drunk.

I clean him up and fall back into my seat, a satisfied smile on my lips.

"I could have killed us."

"But you didn't."

"Are you sure it wasn't you that kissed that stranger tonight?"

I shake my head. "Noel kissed him," I say with a sigh. "And I thought about doing that to you."

"Remind me to be your chauffeur more often."

LAUGHING. I CAN hear laughing, and it only makes my headache worse.

I lift my head from the pillow on Jace's bed and frown. Carl is curled up next to me, purring and kneading the bedding with his one front paw.

"'Morning," I say to him before I walk to the bathroom and pee longer than I ever have before. "That's what drinking that much does to you."

I frown and find some leggings and a loose sweatshirt and, without brushing my hair or my teeth, I venture out to see who Jace is laughing with.

I hope I don't regret looking like this.

I pad barefoot to the kitchen and rub my eyes as Jace and Levi both look over at me with wide smiles.

"What?"

"Good morning, baby," Jace says as he crosses to me and kisses my head. "Want some coffee?"

"Yeah." I yawn and sit next to Levi at the island. "Why are you laughing?"

"I was telling him about you guys last night," Jace says and looks at me with mischievous eyes as he passes me my coffee. "There was a lot of butt plug talk."

I frown, thinking back on last night, then smile. "Oh, yeah. That was funny."

"How do you feel?" Levi asks.

"Like roadkill," I say and take a sip of coffee. "And like you're both yelling at me."

"Not yelling," Jace says. "I was just telling Levi that I got us tickets to see Hamilton on Friday."

"I didn't know Hamilton was in town," I say. "But, yay! I've been wanting to see it."

"I know. I got us really good seats, and we'll have to dress up."

I frown. I have lots of dresses that I could wear, but he's seen them all already. I want to look better for this, it's an actual date.

I'll call Noel and ask her to go shopping with me.

"You don't want to go?" Jace asks, pulling me out of my thoughts.

"What? No, I do. Why do you ask?"

"You're frowning."

"Oh. I'm just hung-over." I sip more coffee and feel it dribble onto my sweatshirt. "And clumsy."

"You're cute when you're hung-over," Levi says with a smile.

"Your flattery will get you everywhere," I reply. "Also, I have questions for you."

"Okay, shoot."

"What happened with you and Starla?"

And just like that, Levi shuts down. He gazes down into his own coffee mug, and his lips tighten.

"Come on, you can tell me. I don't have to know all the dirty specifics, I just want to know if you're going to see her again."

"Not talking about it."

He's literally shut down.

"I'm a vault," I promise him, holding up two fingers. I've never been a scout, and I'm not sure that Girl Scouts hold up two fingers. "I'm not a gossip. Was the sex good? Are you going to see her soon? Do you talk via text all day and fall asleep while talking on the FaceTime?"

"Jesus, you could be a detective," Levi mumbles into his mug before taking a sip. "I'm not talking about Starla, Joy."

"Oh, did it not go well?" I ask and tsk in sympathy. "I'm sorry. Maybe the sex just wasn't all that good."

He glares at me, and I know I'm way off the mark there.

It was good.

"Or maybe she just doesn't have time for a commitment because she's on tour all the time. You know how it is, there's got to be a new guy in every city."

Now his cheeks redden, and I know I've hit a sore spot.

"Cut him some slack," Jace says. "He doesn't want to talk about it."

I ignore Jace, still focused on Levi. "You know, you're my favorite." I lay my hand on his shoulder and pat it. "And I'm your friend. You can talk it out."

"I'm not your favorite," he scoffs.

"Always have been," I swear, holding up my two fingers again, but he just shakes his head and drains his mug, then stands.

"See you later, man."

"You know you want to tell me!" I yell after him, but he just waves and leaves. "Well, that wasn't helpful."

"You know, I never used to be jealous of the way you flirt with my brother," Jace says, catching my attention.

"I don't flirt with him."

"You always have, Joy."

I scowl and stare at him, blinking slowly. "No, I'm just friendly, and I try to draw him out of his stoic shell. He's always so serious."

"It's okay," he says with a pretend sigh. "I'll just have to get used to the flirting, I guess."

"I don't flirt with him, you jackass."

He laughs and drinks *my* coffee.

"Hey! That's mine."

"That's what you get for flirting with my brother."

"I'm going to—"

"What?" he asks, his whole face lit up with humor. "What are you going to do, Joyful?"

He hasn't called me that since college. I hated it then, too.

"I broke you of saying that."

"*Broke* me?"

"Yes. I trained you to *not* call me that."

He shakes his head. "Well, *Joyful*, it looks like I've been *un*trained."

"No more blowjobs in the car for you, my friend."

He stops short, staring at me. "That's just cruel."

"You get what you give." I shrug and give him a look that says *"I don't make the rules."*

"Now, I should take a shower and get this hangover washed off of me. I have to pick Angela up from the clinic today and take her and the puppies home. What have I done? I don't have time for puppies."

"I'll help," he says as he follows me back to the bedroom. "And we have babysitters for when we need them."

"I need a puppy nanny," I mutter as I whip my sweatshirt over my head and toss it on the bed. "And a lobotomy, because I'm clearly crazy."

"No lobotomy," Jace says as he wraps his arms around me from behind, palming my breasts. "Can I take a shower with you?"

"Do you promise to be good?"

"Not a fucking chance."

"Okay, then."

twelve

Joy

"This is the best day *ever*," Noel says as we walk into Neiman's. She looks like a kid on Christmas morning.

I look like I'm headed to the guillotine for a crime I didn't commit.

"This is hell on Earth," I mutter as I trudge behind her, barely looking at the clothes on the racks. "Maybe I should just wear a dress that I already have."

"No, you said yourself, he's seen all of those multiple times. This is a real date, and it should be something nice. Sexy. Alluring."

I roll my eyes behind my sister's back. "That's a little dramatic. I really just don't want to suck."

"You're going to take his breath away," she promises me as she leads me into the evening gown section, and we comb through rack after rack of sparkles, silk, and satin in all colors of the rainbow. Within three minutes, I'm completely overwhelmed.

Noel has four dresses draped over her arm and hurries to find a sales girl.

"We need a dressing room, please."

"Of course. I'm Claire, and I can help with anything you need."

I want to apologize to Claire ahead of time for my sister's over-exuberance and my lack of interest, but I keep my mouth shut and follow the woman into a dressing room.

"Do you need any help?" she asks me.

"No, thanks." Getting in and out of a formal gown is old hat to me after years of attending functions with Jace.

I strip out of my sundress, already prepared by wearing a strapless bra, and reach for the first gown.

It's black and has a tapered hem, starting mid-thigh in the front and skimming my heels in the back.

It also makes my boobs look nonexistent.

"You have to show me every one," Noel calls through the door.

"Even if it sucks?"

"Yes. I have to know *how* it sucks so I can find you something that doesn't suck."

I open the door, and Noel covers her mouth with her hand, her eyes going wide as she cringes.

"Yeah, that's not you."

"Not unless I'm a twelve-year-old boy who loves to dress in drag."

She giggles and flips her hand at me, gesturing me back into the room. "Next."

I can't get out of the black number fast enough and change into a red dress that rests on one shoulder with a giant rose.

Aside from the ugly rose, it's not bad. It hugs my curves in all the right places.

When I open the door, Noel nods, tapping her lips with her finger. "I like it."

"This rose is gaudy."

She nods again. "I agree, but the fit of the dress is great. Is it comfortable?"

"Are these dresses *ever* comfortable?"

"Good point. Try the blush-colored one. I think it might be a winner."

I do as she asks and shimmy into the light pink dress. It's sleeveless but has straps on my shoulders, and a V-cut that dips down past my cleavage. I have to strip out of my bra altogether.

When I walk out of the room, Noel gasps and her eyes fill with tears.

"If Jace reacts like that, this will all be worth it."

"Joy," she breathes. "That dress was made for you. The color is stunning, and the way it dips between your breasts? Jesus, I wish I had boobs like you."

"And I wish I had breasts like you," I reply with a wry grin. Noel's curves are *kicking*. "But I agree. I love this one. I think I'll need some dress tape to keep it in place around my boobs, but otherwise, it's great. Wait, how much is it?"

She rolls her eyes. "You can afford it, no matter how much it is."

"That doesn't mean I'm not concerned with how much it costs."

She just shakes her head and shoos me back into the room. "It doesn't matter, it's yours. Go change so we can go to the shoe department."

I walk into the room and unzip the dress. "I already have shoes," I call out to her.

"Not for that dress."

"Black heels go with everything."

"No," she says, her voice hard. "They don't. They definitely don't go with that dress. You need *nude* heels, and I know there are some Jimmy Choos downstairs that will be divine."

"Who the hell is Jimmy Choo?" I mutter to myself as I slip my sundress back over my head and check the price of the gown, almost swallowing my tongue when I see the tag.

"Noel!"

"What? What's wrong?"

"This dress is *two thousand* dollars."

"Oh, good, so it's not too bad."

I stomp out of the fitting room and stare at my sister in horror. "Not too bad? It's almost the same as my mortgage payment, Noel."

She doesn't even bat an eye. "I will not have you going on this date in anything less than something amazing. You can afford this dress, and it's *gorgeous*. Jace is going to fight a hard-on all night."

Okay, so the thought of *that* makes me happy. Ridiculously happy. I used to want to look nice for Jace because I didn't want to embarrass him in front of his important colleagues.

Now, I just want him to be unable to resist me and think I'm the sexiest woman in the universe.

My, how times have changed.

"Okay, we'll take the dress."

"And no bitching about how much the shoes are," she warns me. "Because they're going to be hella expensive, and totally worth it."

"Gird your loins," I whisper to my credit card and prepare myself for the shopping shitstorm that's about to happen. "I wonder how Jace is doing with the puppies?"

"They can't even walk yet," Noel reminds me. "They just eat and sleep, and their mama does pretty much the same, so I'd say he's fine. He's a surgeon, after all."

I laugh as we take my shopping bag down to the shoe department. "You know, being a surgeon doesn't mean that he's stellar at *everything*."

"Is there something he's not good at?" she asks. I have to really think about it.

"He was never good at writing papers."

"Life stuff," she says. "Is there any life stuff that he sucks at?"

"He's not a great cook, but he doesn't *suck*. I know. He's a really bad bowler."

She smirks. "I stand corrected."

"HOLY FUCK, WE'RE not going anywhere."

And . . . all of the shopping torture was completely worth it. Jace is standing on the other side of my threshold in a black suit that molds to his body, wearing a grey tie. The suit isn't one I've seen before, so it looks as if he went shopping, too. That makes me smile.

The way his grey eyes roam up and down my body leaves me flushed and turned on.

My God, he's hot.

"Come on in." I step back and close the door behind him, then move to get my clutch. But Jace hooks his hand on my waist and pulls me against him.

"I'm serious, I want to strip this magnificent dress off you and fuck you into next week."

"We have tickets," I remind him softly against his lips. "And dinner reservations."

"I don't give a shit."

"I might get naked for you later," I say before I kiss him quickly. "But it's a first date, so we'll see. I'm not usually that kind of girl."

"This isn't our first date," he says, furrowing his brow.

"Everything before was as friends," I remind him, then step away to grab my clutch and check on Angela. She's just been outside, has eaten, and is in the whelping box with her babies.

"I should have brought you flowers," he mumbles with a frown.

"You're forgiven," I reply. "Dad's going to stop by in a couple of hours to check on Angela, so she and the babies should be fine."

"Let's go before I talk you into staying." He holds his arm out for me to take and escorts me to his car. We drive into the city, leave the car with a valet, and walk into a restaurant I've never been to before. It's fancy—maybe the most opulent I've ever been.

Once we're seated and given our menus, our waiter appears to take our drink order.

"A bottle of champagne for the table," Jace says, smiling at me. He knows I love the bubbly. "And we'll start with the oysters."

"Yes, sir," the waiter says, bowing before leaving us to look over the menu.

"Aren't you fancy?" I say with a grin.

"I want you to have a good time."

"I already am," I reply and reach over to squeeze his hand. "Thank you in advance for tonight."

He lifts my hand to his lips, keeping his gaze on mine as he kisses my knuckles. "I don't think I've ever seen anything as beautiful as you are tonight."

"How can you fluster me after all these years?"

"I could ask you the same question."

The waiter returns and makes a show of popping the cork on the champagne, pouring us each a glass and setting the bottle in a tall ice bucket at the side of the table.

The Cristal has just the right amount of bubble, tickling my nose as I take the first sip.

"That's a new suit," I comment as I peruse the menu. "You look quite handsome in it."

"Thank you," he says with a smile. "I went shopping with Noel."

I lower my menu and stare at him in surprise. "No way."

"It's true. I wanted something new, and Lia was busy. Noel was excited to go." I giggle, and he tips his head to the side, watching me. "What's so funny?"

"My sister is a piece of work." I sip my champagne. "She took *me* shopping for this dress. She basically arranged our entire wardrobe for tonight."

He smirks. "Sounds like her."

"We'll have to get a photo and send it to her."

"Deal." He returns his attention to the menu, and when we've both decided on what we want, the waiter returns to take our order.

"Any word—" I begin but am interrupted by a tall brunette

woman in a shockingly red dress with a slit up to the side of her hip. Her lips are painted the same red hue, and her blue eyes are pinned on Jace as she sets her hand on his shoulder and smiles.

"Jace, so lovely to see you."

"Hello, Maria. This is—"

"I haven't seen you around the hospital lately," she says, clearly not interested in who I am.

"No," he says, shaking his head. "I've been on leave."

"Well, hopefully not for too long," she says with a wink. "We need to arrange for another romp in the supply closet."

Her blue eyes rake over him, from his face to his shoulders and dipping lower.

This isn't like the girl flirting with him at the grocery store. No, that was harmless and even funny.

This isn't funny.

He fucked her.

"Not going to happen, Maria," he says, the smile gone from his face. "This is Joy, my girlfriend."

"We'll see," she says, winks, then walks away, her hips swaying in her tight dress.

Before either of us can say anything at all, the waiter arrives with our dinner. He places the plates before us, offers freshly ground pepper, and tops off our champagne. I immediately drink half of my glass.

Jace's eyes are pinned to mine, apology and anger shining in their depths. And frankly, I don't know how I feel.

Embarrassed, which is stupid because I don't have anything to be embarrassed about. I'm surprised. And I suppose, reminded that I don't know everything there is to know about Jace and his past.

Once the waiter is gone, neither of us reaches for our utensils to eat. I'm still sipping my drink, and Jace just watches me, his chest rising and falling as he breathes.

"I owe you an apology."

"Why?" I ask, setting my glass down and reaching for my fork to dig into my chicken Alfredo. "Have you fucked her since we've been together?"

"Of course, not," he says with a scowl.

"Well, then, you don't have anything to apologize for." I take a bite. "Because if we need to be sorry for every person we've slept with since we were nineteen, tonight isn't the time for that."

He narrows his eyes, and his hands curl into fists on the table. "No. It isn't."

I swallow hard and take another sip of my drink. "It's also not your fault that she's a bitch. And rude. That's on her."

"You're entirely too calm about this."

"Why?"

"Because if a man you'd been with had done what she did, I would have laid him out flat."

I smile before taking another bite of my meal. "Well, I might have given a thought to breaking the hand that touched you."

"That would have ruined her day," he says, finally taking a bite of his own dinner. "And maybe her career as a surgeon."

The fact that she's a surgeon only twists the knife in my chest. I'm successful in my own right, and I don't need to compare myself to her, but *damn it.*

"Do you want to talk about it?" he asks.

"Do *you*?"

"I'd like to clarify some things so we can get on with our

evening," he says with a nod. "Because now it's awkward, and that pisses me off."

"Okay." I wipe my mouth with a napkin. "Tell me."

Jace reaches over for the bottle of champagne and fills my glass, instinctively knowing that I probably need it.

He's right.

"She's a surgeon at the hospital, and I've had sex with her exactly twice."

"When was the last time?" I ask, holding my breath and watching his face, which doesn't change in the slightest.

"Almost a year ago," he replies immediately and reaches for my hand. "You're right, we don't need to go into who we've been with in the past. It might kill me. But she gave me no choice because she was rude to you, disrespectful, and made a show of touching me."

"Really wishing I'd broken that hand," I reply and then smile at him. His face is tense with worry, which only makes me love him more. "We're fine, Jace. Really."

"I'll always be honest," he says. "I don't have secrets from you."

"I know."

It's true. We don't have secrets, and we don't lie to each other. It's one of the things I love the most about our relationship.

"My trust for you isn't an issue," I assure him. "My man is hot, I know that. I'm secure enough to not fly into a jealous rage every time someone hits on you."

"You could fly into a *tiny* jealous rage," he says with a laugh, the tension easing from his face. "It's kind of hot."

"I didn't know what to do," I admit. "The grocery store was easy. She didn't do anything wrong. She saw a handsome guy and said hi. *This* woman was a different story. But she's gone. *I* have the guy, and if she pulls anything again, I'll punch her in the cunt."

His eyes bulge, and he chokes on the bite of food he just took, making me smile smugly.

"I don't think I've ever heard you say that word before."

"We're both full of surprises, aren't we?"

"THAT WAS *AMAZING*," I announce as we pull up to my house. The light on the porch is on, signaling that my dad was here to check on Angela and the puppies. "Seriously, all of the hype is well worth it."

"Agreed," he says with a grin as he follows me up to the front door. I reach out to unlock it, but he turns me to him, and right there on my porch, he grips my shoulders and lowers his mouth to mine, nibbling the corner of my lips seductively.

My knees are weak. My panties are soaked, and my nipples are hard and pressed against the fabric of my dress.

He kisses along my jawline to my ear, tugs the lobe with his teeth, and whispers, "Are you going to invite me in?"

"I didn't know you needed an invitation." I swallow hard, unable to take a deep breath. Jesus, he's potent.

"It's our first date," he reminds me.

"Right." I swallow again just before he drags his tongue along my lower lip. His hands roam over my back and move down to my ass, then slide up again, making it difficult to think. "Jace, would you like to come inside?"

"Very much." He grins as I reach behind me for the handle,

open the door, and stumble inside. I'm so turned on, I'm clumsy.

I set my clutch on the table by the door, then immediately tend to Angela. She's whining, wanting to go outside. Once she's back in and snuggled up to her babies, I turn to find Jace leaning his hip on the island countertop, his jacket already off, and his arms crossed over his chest.

"Is she taken care of?"

"Yeah."

He nods, his eyes holding mine, and I've never been so nervous to be with him in my life. He's suddenly taller, broader, more *imposing* than I remember. And the look in his eyes says we're about to have a night that I'll never forget.

He crosses to me and drags his fingertips up and down my upper arms, spreading goosebumps over my entire body. His fingers graze my collarbone and move up my neck until he's cradling my face in his hands. I'm completely under his spell.

"You're gorgeous, Joy."

"So are you," I breathe.

"I just have one request." His lips brush mine softly. I'd promise him *anything* in this moment.

"What is it?"

"Take. This. Off."

thirteen

Jace

She's tempted me all night. The dress skims over her curves deliciously, showing off her cleavage. I've wanted to kiss her there.

So, I do.

She gasps as I drag my tongue over her sternum and up her neck.

"Keep the heels on," I whisper against her lips before claiming them, teasing her with light kisses then deep ones, tangling my tongue with hers.

She peels the dress over her shoulders, and it drops to pool around her feet. She's braless, wearing only a tiny scrap of lace as panties.

"I want to boost you onto this countertop and fuck you," I inform her. A shiver rolls through her, and she nods, her mouth seeking mine as I lift her into my arms. "But I'm not going to."

"Sad," she pouts, making me grin.

"We need the bed for what I have in store."

Her eyes flare with anticipation and need as I climb her

stairs with her in my arms. When I reach her bed, I set her on her feet next to it.

"You're too . . . dressed," she informs me, but I catch her hands before they can unfasten my tie. Her eyes jump to mine as I kiss her fingertips.

"This is all about *you*."

"Then I want *you* naked," she insists, and I bite her fingertip, making her pupils dilate.

"I think you'll be doing what you're told tonight, my love."

She doesn't argue. Her pink lips part on a soft gasp, and as she stands before me, I drag my hands down her sides to catch the lace at her hips with my thumbs, then peel the panties down her legs. She kicks out of them. She's finally naked, aside from the heels on her feet. I kiss her ankle and up the outside of her leg, my hand grazing the inside of the same thigh as I move, and smile when I find a she's soaking wet between her legs.

"Good girl," I whisper before planting an open-mouthed kiss on her hip. "This right here, Joy?"

"Mm-hmm?"

"This curvy hip is mine."

She bites her lip, watching me as if she's in a trance as I kiss my way over her belly to her navel and circle it with my nose. I push my fingers inside her and then still, simply filling her as my mouth feasts on her flesh.

"Sit," I command. She follows orders well, scooting back on the bed until I'm kneeling between her legs, my fingers still inside her, and her heels planted on the linens. "Do you have any idea what you did to me tonight?"

She shakes her head no. "Tell me."

"You make me lose myself," I murmur, kissing up her belly

to one perfect breast, the nipple tight and straining toward the ceiling. "Your body makes me ache." I pluck the nipple with my lips. "I have a constant hard-on."

"You're welcome," she whispers with a smile, and I tug the nipple again, harder this time, making her catch her breath.

"These breasts are mine, Joy."

She nods wordlessly, and I make my way to the cleavage she's had on display all night, dragging my nose down her smooth skin, then licking my way back up again. Her hips writhe, trying to make my fingers move and release the pressure I'm sure is building within her.

But I don't oblige her yet. I will, in spades, just not quite yet.

"I fucking love your mouth," I murmur against her lips, brushing against them softly. "Your lips are full and beautiful. And they feel so fucking good around my cock."

She sticks out her tongue to brush my lower lip, and I about come in my pants.

Fuck me, she unarms me.

"This mouth is mine."

"All yours," she agrees before I lower my weight atop her, kissing her until we're both breathless, then kissing her again. Her hands make their way into my hair, holding on tightly as she sighs, and I sink in deeper.

I make a come-here motion with my fingers, moving them inside her for the first time, and Joy's hips jerk off the bed as she gasps and pulls on my hair.

"Oh, God."

"So wet," I whisper and trail my mouth down her jawline. "So tight. Have I mentioned how much I love your pussy?"

"Not today," she manages, panting and writhing beneath me.

"Your pussy is what dreams are made of," I tell her as I add my thumb to her clit and she cries out, giving in to the first orgasm of the evening, her body quaking and clenching around me. "And guess what it is?"

"Yours?"

"That's right, baby. It's mine." I kiss down her body, moving quickly to replace my hand with my mouth. As soon as my tongue pushes inside her, she explodes again, crying out my name. "Good girl."

"I can't do any more," she pants as she comes down from the high.

"Oh, you can. And you will." I hurry to shrug out of my clothes, cursing myself for not doing it earlier because all I can think of now is sinking inside her until I'm blind. I kiss her leg, the underside of her knee, and smile when she whimpers. "Another hot spot?"

"My whole body is a fucking hot spot," she says, her voice filled with confusion and frustration. "How do you do this to me?"

"It's us, Joy." Naked now, I cover her and cradle her head in my hands as I ease inside her as slowly as possible, giving her a moment to adjust to me. "I can guarantee you that it's never been like this with anyone else."

"Never," she agrees, watching me with hot eyes as I bury myself balls-deep and brush my nose back and forth over hers. She hitches her knees up around my sides, spreading herself wider and making me sink farther into her.

"I don't know where I end, and you begin anymore. And I'm not just talking about this."

"I know," she says, digging her nails into my shoulders as I begin to move. "I know."

I link my fingers with hers and stretch our hands above her head, holding her down as I move in long, slow strokes, building us both toward orgasm. She pants, giving as good as she gets.

"Mine," I growl, staring down into her eyes. "You. Are. Mine. All of you, every day."

"Yes," she says and arches her neck, drowning in her orgasm as another wave pulls her under. Her muscles bear down and milk me, and I can't hold back any longer. I bury my face in her neck and grunt with my release.

"Mine," I whisper before kissing her neck and letting go of her hands. She frames my face and smiles up at me.

"And you're mine."

"KNOCK-KNOCK."

I glance over at the front door, happily surprised to find Joy's dad, Larry, standing at the screen, smiling at me. Nancy is sitting patiently at his side.

"Hey, come on in," I call over. "Joy's at work, but she should be home shortly."

"I came to look in on this sweet girl," he says as he looks into Angela's whelping box and reaches in to pet the new mother behind the ears. "Look how pretty you are there. How are these babies doing?"

"Now I know where Joy gets her love of animals," I say, wiping my hand on a towel.

"Never met an animal I didn't like," Larry agrees as he stands up, holding one of the puppies. Nancy sniffs and strains to see, so he shows her the little baby, then gives it a kiss on the head before giving it back to Angela. "I'm also glad that Joy isn't here because I'd like to have a conversation with you."

"Oh?" I cock a brow and toss the towel onto the countertop. "Would you like a beer?"

"Better not. I'm driving, and I'm a cheap date these days." He chuckles and sits with me in the living room. "I hate to be a cliché, but I'm afraid I'm going to be anyway. I'd like to know what your intentions are with my daughter."

I cross one ankle over a knee and take a deep breath. I've been thinking about this a *lot* lately. Hell, it's *all* I think about. So, I'm confident when I hold his gaze with mine and reply, "I'm going to marry her."

His eyes widen, and his whole face lights up. "When did you ask her?"

"Well, I haven't yet. I should say, I *want* to marry her."

"Why in the hell haven't you asked?"

I stand now, too keyed up to sit, and pace the room. "Because I feel like I should wait until this mess with the hospital is cleared up. How can I offer Joy a future when I don't know for sure what that future looks like?"

"Well, you're not psychic, son. None of us knows what it looks like. Do you really think her love for you would change based on the outcome of the case?"

I turn and stare at him, surprised that he'd ask me that. "Of course, not."

"Then I'll ask again, what are you waiting for?"

I open my mouth, then close it again, and shrug. "I don't know. I already bought her a ring, I've just been waiting for the right time."

"Then you're *wasting* time," he says sadly. "Trust me when I say, there is less time in life than you'll ever want. It's never enough. I'd give anything to have just ten minutes back with my Elizabeth."

"I know."

"And you have the love of your life at your fingertips. If you want to marry her, marry her."

"You make it sound so easy."

"It is." He shrugs. "I don't see where it's difficult. That girl loves you like crazy."

"I know."

"Elizabeth and I knew from the day Joy brought you home all those years ago. You both insisted that you were just friends, but when you left that night, Elizabeth looked at me with that soft smile she had and said, 'He's the one for her.'"

I swallow hard, unsure what to say.

"She just knew things like that," he continues. "She was usually right."

"I'm sorry she's not here."

He nods once. "Me too, Jace. You have no idea. So, you marry my girl, and you have babies and enjoy every damn day of your life with her. You won't find better than her."

"I know it."

"Daddy," Joy says as she comes inside. She's carrying files and breathing hard, and I know she didn't hear anything before coming through the door. Joy isn't one to hover. If she wanted to know what we were saying, she would have come in and asked.

"What are you doing?"

"Just chatting with Jace," Larry says. "I came to look in on Angela."

"She's doing great," Joy says with a smile, but it's strained, and I want to know what's wrong. "Some of the babies' eyes are opening."

"I saw that," Larry says and smiles as Joy squats to give Nancy all of the belly rubs in the world.

"Oh, I've missed you, sweet girl." Nancy grunts in delight. "Yes, I have. How are you, baby girl? Her eye looks good."

"Yep, everything has been just fine," Larry says with a grin. "She might have gained a pound because she likes table scraps."

"You shouldn't feed her people food," Joy says, not looking up from the bulldog. "But I'm sure she loves it."

"We should go," Larry says.

"Oh, you don't want to stay for dinner?"

"No, I have chili on the stove at home. I just came to say hello."

Joy gives her dad a big hug before Larry and Nancy leave. She falls onto the couch and sighs.

"Not a good day?" I ask.

"I had to send a tech home because she caught the flu from another tech, who came to work with it last week," she says and rubs her hands over her face. "So, we've been short-handed, and of course, it's a full moon, so we're busier than normal."

"So that's not just a people hospital thing?" I say, sitting next to her and pulling her into my arms so I can kiss her head and give her a cuddle.

"No, I think it's a medical thing, regardless of the species," she says. "What's for dinner? Please tell me I don't have to cook."

"Chinese takeout. It's on the way."

"You're the best boyfriend ever."

"I know." I kiss her head again.

I'm aiming for being the best husband ever.

"HI, SUSAN, IT'S Joy," Joy says into her phone from the bed. She's curled in a ball, under the covers. They're even pulled up over her head.

I fucking hate it when she's sick. I can open up a chest and *replace* a heart, but I can't save her from the flu.

It's fucking ridiculous.

"I've succumbed to the flu," she croaks into the phone. "Throwing up like crazy. Uh-huh. No, I'm not pregnant."

That gives me pause.

"I have chills and aches and a fever, Susan. It's the flu. Can you call Dr. Miller and ask her to fill in for me today? Thanks. I'll check in tomorrow morning."

She hangs up, and suddenly her phone is flung out from under the covers, but she's still hiding under there.

In the past, the idea of a woman I was with being pregnant would have filled my stomach with lead and my heart with dread, but the thought of *Joy* being round with my baby isn't horrible at all.

I want her to be my *wife*. I want to have a family with her, endure the sleepless nights and the diapers and everything else that goes along with it.

"I'm dying."

"I'm sorry, baby." I rush into the bathroom and wet a washcloth with cold water, then take it back to her and peel back the covers to find her sweaty beneath them. "You have a fever. Where's your thermometer?"

"Bathroom cabinet," she says, holding the cloth to her forehead. "Why do they bring this shit to work? I give them sick days so they will *take* them when they're sick, not cash them out at the end of the year. I think I have to stop offering that option. If you don't use your sick time, you lose it."

"They'll call in when they're *not* sick."

"But they'll call when they *are,* and that's the point because this is bullshit."

I stick the thermometer in her ear and pull it back out. "Just over one hundred."

"At least it's not too bad," she says with a sigh. "I'll sleep it off and be better tomorrow."

"If you're lucky." I lean down to kiss her, but she recoils.

"You can't kiss me. You need a mask. I don't want you to get sick."

"I won't," I promise her, but she shakes her head adamantly.

"No kissing. And you can't sleep with me. You should probably just go home until this blows over."

"When pigs fly," I mutter. "Go to sleep, babe. I'll take care of Angela and get you some soup."

At the mention of food, her eyes widen in terror, and she makes a run for the bathroom, hurling her guts out.

I wring out the washcloth and press it to her neck as she dry heaves, her whole body lifting.

"Poor baby," I murmur, rubbing her back in circles. "I hate this."

"Me, too," she whimpers. "No food for now, okay?"

"No, it seems you can't tolerate it yet, but I am getting some water and apple juice. You can sip it."

"Okay."

"I can't have you dehydrated."

"Okay."

"Do you want me to find something on Netflix for you?"

"No, I want to sleep," she whispers, leaning on her forearm, still poised over the toilet. I pull her into my arms and carry her back to the bed, but before I put her under the covers, I change her clothes into something cleaner and more comfortable, get a fresh washcloth, then tuck her in.

Before I can leave to fetch the water, she tugs on my hand, pulling me in for a hug.

"Thank you, Dr. Crawford. It's handy having a doctor around when you don't feel good."

"I feel absolutely worthless," I mutter. "If you needed bypass surgery, I could do that no problem. I'm not good at this part."

"You're amazing," she says. "And I'm grateful. It sucks to be sick and alone, so thanks for sticking around."

"Nowhere else I'd rather be, sweetheart. Now, let me get Angela outside and grab you some water."

I tuck her in and hurry out of the room. I have one set of linens that she's already sweated through in the wash, so I throw those into the dryer on my way downstairs. I let Angela outside and check on the puppies, who are starting to roam around the box and make more noise. They're adorable. Before long, though, they won't want to be confined to their pen.

With Angela back in with her pups, I grab a bottle of water and a glass of juice and hurry back up to the bedroom. Joy isn't in bed.

I set the provisions down and find her wrapped around the toilet, asleep on her arms.

Poor baby.

I lift her again and tuck her into bed. She doesn't even wake up.

With her sleeping, I set to work cleaning the toilet and the rest of the bathroom. I don't know how long she'll be sick, and if she's going to spend most of the time kneeling in front of the toilet, it should be clean for her.

I shake my head as I kneel to hand-mop behind the toilet. If you'd told me a year ago that this is what I'd be doing on a Tuesday afternoon rather than saving a life in surgery, I would have called you a liar.

But I'm not sorry. I hate the circumstances, but it's been awesome getting to know Joy in a different way and falling in love with her. Being with her almost every day.

She's everything good in this world.

And she's mine.

fourteen

Joy

"It's been *three days*," I say into the phone to my doctor.

"The flu can take five to ten days to run its course," she reminds me. "And at this point, it's too late for an anti-viral. You need to just let it run its course."

"I have a business to run," I grumble. "I have patients."

"And you can't do them any good when you're sick. Stay in bed, get plenty of fluids, eat what you can handle. Make sure you watch that fever."

"Okay." I sigh. I already know all of this.

"If you get worse, come into the urgent care. The flu sucks, it's inconvenient, but it can be dangerous, so make sure you're watching yourself."

"I will," I promise. "Thanks."

Actually, I'm not watching myself, Jace is watching me. And he's been hovering like a worried mother hen.

It was sweet at first, but as of this morning, it crossed over into annoying. So, I shooed him out the door to his house to work on some projects with Levi and Wyatt. He put up a bit of a fight, but I think he was relieved to get out for a while, and not be on nurse duty.

I can't blame him. I'm going stir-crazy, and I'm the sick one.

I've moved my "sick station" as I call it down to the couch in the living room. This way, I can keep an eye on Angela and the babies.

Carl's been following me around for the past few days, hovering as much as Jace does. But he doesn't nag me to drink my water.

Angela jumps out of her box, leaving her pups to nap alone, and cuddles up with me on the couch.

"You're a sweet girl," I croon to her and smile when she kisses my chin. "Yes, you're just a lover."

She sighs and lays across my lap, falling asleep almost instantly. Carl is curled up on the top of the couch where he can watch over us from his perch.

I wasn't lying to Jace the other day when I told him it sucks to be sick and alone. So, I call Noel and ask her to come keep me company.

She arrives thirty minutes later, with warm broth and more saltine crackers.

"Hey," she says when she walks in and sees the three of us on the couch. "You don't look so good."

"I don't feel good," I reply, scowling. "Here, put this on."

She scowls at the face mask in my hand.

"No way."

"Seriously, you need to wear this so you don't get sick."

"*You* called *me*," she says, shaking her head as she sets the broth and crackers on the coffee table, then sits across the room from me on a chair, sans mask. "I'll be over here, out of the germ zone."

"Noel."

"Joy," she mimics, and I narrow my eyes at her, making her laugh. "Tell me about your date the other night."

"First of all, nice suit you chose," I say, and she grins without denying that she took Jace shopping. "He looked hot in it."

"Right? So hot. You're welcome. Tell me everything."

"Dinner was delicious and eventful." I tell her all about the woman stopping at our table, ignoring me and hitting on Jace.

"Bitch," Noel says with a scowl. "I'm surprised you didn't trip her."

"Well, I thought about it, but I don't think that was her first rodeo. She knew exactly what she was doing, and how it would make everyone at the table feel."

"Tramp," Noel mutters. "I just don't understand. Why are women so horrible to each other? Why are they so desperate to tear each other down? Because that's exactly what that is, desperation."

"I don't know. I mean, if it were me, and I'd had a couple of romps with Jace and had a crush on him but saw that he was with someone else, I might have said hi, but I wouldn't have made a big production of it like that."

"Of course, not," she says. "And if she thinks that's the way to make men come running to her, well, she's not very good at this."

"That's just it, *do* men go for that sort of thing? Because it was not sexy to me, and Jace was *pissed*."

"As he should be."

"But maybe some men would think it's hot?"

"If they do, they're not the men we want putting their

penises in our vaginas," she says with a sigh. "How was the show?"

"So good. Totally lives up to the hype. The rest of the evening was a lot of fun."

"Good, I'm glad she didn't ruin it for you."

"It's not his fault, although he did apologize. And he felt the need to tell me about her, I guess to get it all out in the open."

"That's good. Even though I'm sure you didn't want to know much, it's good that he doesn't feel like he has something to hide, or that he doesn't want you to be privy to everything."

"I'd rather he be honest, yes," I agree. "So, that's about it."

"That's *it*? The outfits I picked out didn't lead to some earth-rocking sex?"

"Well, yeah. That happened." I shrug a shoulder. "But I'm not telling you about it."

"Damn. Well, should we just watch some Netflix then?"

"Let's do it."

I'M *FINALLY* FEELING better.

It seems the fourth day is the charm. I'm still stuck at home, but I'm not throwing up, the fever is gone, and I'm only a little achy.

I'll take it.

But I *am* suffering from cabin fever. Jace came and spent the night with me again last night, but I encouraged him to go back to his place today to continue working on his projects. We don't know how long he'll be off work, so he should get as much done as he can, and babysitting me isn't productive.

Especially now that I'm not helpless anymore.

Angela has been hopping in and out of her box. The puppies are more restless, wanting to roam around and play. In another week, I'll be weaning them off their mother's milk and giving them puppy food.

I can't believe how quickly they grow.

"Hey, girl," I say to Angela as she comes to my side and nudges my leg, wanting some love. "Do you have some cabin fever, too? Maybe we should go for a walk."

Some fresh air sounds just perfect, so I grab a leash and my sweatshirt, and we're off, on the same route that I used to take Nancy on.

I have no doubt that Angela will learn the route in time. She has a tendency to pull on the leash, so I have to take my time, teaching her how to behave. But by the time we're headed back to the house, she's calmed down and is walking by my side.

Yes, she's going to be a snap to train. German Shepherds are highly intelligent. It's why they're such good service and police dogs.

Just as I walk through the door and Angela scrambles over to her box to check on the pups, my phone rings.

"Hi, Levi."

"Hey, Joy." His voice sounds weird. "Wyatt's in L.A. with Lia, and Mom and Dad are on vacation. Jace won't answer his fucking phone."

"What's wrong?"

"I need a ride," he says grimly. "I've been shot."

My whole world stills. "You've *what*? Are you at the hospital?"

"Yeah, at the ER. I've been discharged, but—"

"I'll be right there."

I hang up on him, grab my keys and purse, and race to the hospital, breaking several speeding laws on the way.

My God, Levi was shot! We always knew this was a possibility, but I never thought it would actually happen. I wonder how bad it is. Is he bleeding too badly? Is he in a coma?

"Jesus, calm down. None of that is the case if they discharged him. And, you talked to him."

I shake my head as I turn into the ER parking lot. I hurry inside and find Levi sitting in a chair in the waiting room. His right jeans' leg has been cut up to his hip, and he has gauze wrapped around his thigh. He stands, and I rush to him.

"Oh, thank God." I wrap my arms around his stomach and hug him tightly. "You're okay."

"I told you I was discharged," he says, patting my back awkwardly. "You can just take me home."

"Like hell," I mutter as he limps beside me out to the car. "I'm not taking you home. You're on painkillers."

"So?"

"So, you shouldn't be alone," I say as I pull out of the parking lot and head toward home. "You'll come stay with me today."

"I don't need a mother," he grumbles. "I just want to go home and fall asleep for about twenty-four hours."

"*I'm* the boss," I reply. "And you'll do what I say. You need to come home with me."

"What if I don't want to?"

"Don't care," I say as if there's no room for argument. "How did it happen?"

"Fucking drug dealers," he murmurs and leans his head against the door. I frown over at him and want to ask more questions, but he's already asleep.

I wonder why he couldn't reach Jace. I'll try to call him when I get home.

But when I turn the corner to my house, Jace's car is in the driveway.

I pull to a stop and reach over to nudge Levi. "Hey, sleepy-head. Wake up. I have a guest room waiting for you."

"Just take me the fuck home."

"No." Not intimidated in the least, I get out and hurry around the car to help Levi from the vehicle. He leans on me as we walk into the house.

"There you are," Jace begins when he sees me, then stops in his tracks at the sight of Levi's arm wrapped around my shoulders. "What the hell happened?"

"He's been shot," I inform him.

"Tried to call you," Levi says.

"I was driving, and the sound was off on my phone," Jace says. "You didn't leave a message."

"Called Joy," he says.

"Those are some good pain meds," I comment as I lead him through the house to the guest room, grateful that it's on the first floor.

"Let me look at it," Jace says, reaching for the bandage on his brother's leg, but Levi shakes his head. "Already had it looked at. Stitched up. I can't even feel it."

"Just wait until those meds wear off, pal," Jace says grimly. "Did the bullet go through?"

"It was a graze," Levi says. "Just took a chunk of flesh out. It'll heal."

"Who did it?"

"Perp," Levi says with a shrug and yawns as he falls onto

the bed. He's snoring before Jace can ask any more questions.

"Damn it," Jace mutters, looking at Levi with worried eyes. "I'm sorry I missed the call."

"It's okay. I'm glad I was around to go get him. I didn't realize your parents were on vacation."

"Belize," he says with a nod. "And Wyatt and Lia left for L.A. this morning."

"That's what he said. I'm going to run upstairs to get my thermometer."

Jace nods, and I rush upstairs and back again in less than twenty seconds. "His temp is normal."

"We'll watch him for fever," Jace says. "But if the hospital cleaned him up, he should be okay."

"We'll watch him anyway," I agree and pat his shoulder. "Let's let him sleep."

"You must be feeling better," he comments as we walk into the kitchen.

"Much better today," I confirm. "I'm just a little tired and achy, especially in my hips." I rub them and rock back and forth. "Probably from all the lying around I did. But I'm not throwing up every ten minutes."

"Thank God." He pulls me in for a big hug and replaces my hands on my hips with his own, rubbing firmly. "I hate it when you're sick. Let's not do that again anytime soon."

"Deal."

"Now we have Levi to take care of, at least for today. And believe me when I say, he's going to be a dick when he wakes up."

"Not good at being injured, huh?"

"No."

"He wanted me to take him home, but I refused. I didn't

think he should be alone on the medication."

"Good call." He sighs and rubs his eyes. "I got a call from the hospital."

"And?"

"I have a meeting with them on Monday morning."

"That's, like, a week away."

"No, it's a few days away," he says with a laugh. "You lost a few days there from being sick. It's Friday afternoon, sweetheart."

"Oh." I frown and shake my head. "Well, that sucks that you have to wait all weekend to find out what's going on."

"What's two more days?" he asks with a shrug. "If you're feeling up to it, I'd like to take you out to dinner tomorrow night."

"Sounds good. In the meantime, I'm fixing tacos tonight."

"Sounds great."

"Real food actually sounds good. I'm taking that as a good sign."

"Me, too." He pulls me in and kisses me soundly for the first time all week. "I've missed you."

"You've been with me every day."

"Not the way I want to be." He tugs me closer and slides his hand over my ass as he presses his erection to my belly.

"Your brother is injured in the other room."

"He's asleep," he reminds me. "Knocked out cold. And we have plenty of time before dinner."

I smile, take his hand, and lead him upstairs. "How will we ever fill the time?"

"I have plenty of ideas, sweetheart."

fifteen

Jace

"I can't believe my car died," Joy grumbles next to me, scowling out the window of my Audi as I drive her to work.

"I don't know why you haven't replaced it yet," I say lightly. "You've had that car forever."

"Six years," she says with a sigh. "I was trying to eke out every drop of life it had."

"I'd say you accomplished that. I can go with you to buy a new one tomorrow."

I have plans for tonight. Big plans. Well, I *will* have big plans after I drop her off.

"I guess I don't have a choice," she says and swallows hard. "Also, isn't this flu supposed to be gone? Why am I still a little nauseated?"

"It can take up to two weeks to make its way through your system." I frown over at her and press my hand to her forehead. No fever. "Maybe you should stay home."

"No." She shakes her head adamantly. "No way. I *need* to

work. I'm sorry, I don't mean to hurt your feelings because of your work situation—"

"I get it," I reply. "Trust me, I get it."

"I'll be fine. I asked Susan to pick up some ginger ale yesterday, and I'll just sip on that. Are you going to be okay with the puppies?"

"Of course." I pull into the parking lot of her clinic and smile at her as she unclips her belt. "Have a good day, dear."

She snorts out a laugh. "I'll call you when I'm ready to come home. It'll probably be around seven."

"Sounds good. Don't forget we're going out for dinner tonight. I love you."

She smiles softly, the way she always does when I tell her I love her. "I love you, too. Have a good day."

And with that, she hurries inside, and I shift into planning mode.

I call Noel, listening to it ring through the speakers of my car as I pull away from the clinic.

"Hello?"

"Hi, Noel, it's Jace."

"What's up?"

"I need your help." I take a deep breath, trying to keep the butterflies at bay. "I need to come up with a plan for this evening."

"For what?"

"I'm going to propose to Joy."

There's silence on the other end. It makes me frown. "Noel?"

"Well, I just think that's the sweetest thing." She sniffles. "I'm so happy for you both. And I'm relieved that you finally came to your senses and realized that you were made for each other."

"Focus," I say with a smile. "I need you to help me come up with a plan."

"Okay. Come over to my house, and we'll figure it out."

"Thanks."

I end the call and drive to Noel's, which isn't too far away from Joy's house. She's waiting on her porch for me with a sappy smile on her face.

"You're going to be my brother-in-law."

"Are you going to be mushy about this? Because you're no help to me like this."

"Hey, my sister only gets engaged once every thirty years or so," she says with a smirk. "Let me enjoy it."

"I was thinking that I could rent a helicopter tour over the Sound or something."

She frowns. "Joy gets motion sick."

"Oh, right." I push my fingers into my eye sockets and sigh. "I knew that. I don't know why this is making me stupid."

"Because you want to get it right, which I think is fantastic. Do you want some coffee?"

"Yes, please."

She brews me a cup, and we're quiet as we try to think of the best way to do this.

"It's raining today," she says.

"I know, which rules out anything outside."

"Don't you have something that you love to do together? Like a favorite restaurant, or something like that?"

"Yeah, but that seems cliché."

"You also can't be cheesy," she says as she sets my coffee in front of me with sugar and cream to doctor it up myself.

I take it black.

"That's why I'm here," I remind her.

"You could send her on a scavenger hunt all over town to places that mean a lot to you both and then you're waiting at the end with the ring." She smiles, pleased with herself.

"I have *today* to figure this out."

"Why did you wait until the last minute?"

"I didn't. I just know that today is the day I want to propose."

"You've had fifteen years to figure this out," she mutters and sighs. "Okay, how about this? You get a prescription bottle, and you have them make a label that says the prescription is *Will You Marry Me?* and that the ailment is love."

I stare at her, blinking. "That's the stupidest thing I've ever heard."

"No! You're both doctors! It makes perfect sense."

"You said I can't get cheesy. That's cheesy as fuck."

She sighs, tapping her lips.

"Okay, you need to get a fishing lure—" she begins, but I stop her, holding my hand up.

"We don't fish, and if you say *this catch is a keeper*, I'll never speak to you again. Think about how *you* would want to be proposed to."

"Well, that's easy. I want to go to Paris, spend the day in the spa where I get my nails done perfectly, and then he takes me to dinner, and we walk around Paris at night, discovering little cafés and watching people kiss. And then we'd end up on a bridge with a view of the Eiffel Tower, and he'd get on one knee and ask me to marry him. He would have hired a professional photographer to secretly follow us and take photos, especially of *the moment*. The ring will be a round cut solitaire, and I'll cry daintily, and of course, say yes."

I stare at her, my mouth open, not sure what to say except, "Shit. I should have planned this sooner."

"That's *my* dream proposal," she reminds me. "This is Joy we're talking about. She wouldn't need or even want all of that. Hell, you could just lie in bed and say, 'let's get hitched' and she'd say, 'okay.'"

I raise my eyebrows, thinking it over. Noel rushes to add, "But do *not* do it that way. You still need to do something sweet that when people ask her how you proposed, she can tell the story and they're like, '*awww!*'"

"This is a lot of fucking pressure," I mutter, rubbing my fingers over my lips.

"I know you have to have a romantic side," she says. "It can be simple *and* romantic all at the same time. What's she doing today?"

"Working. I told her I was going to take her out to dinner tonight."

"She's going to be tired," Noel guesses. "So I suggest doing it at home. Wait! I have an idea."

"I think I've heard enough of your ideas."

"No, this one is really sweet, doesn't involve a passport, and we should be able to pull it together before she gets off of work."

"Okay, I'm all ears."

"HI," JOY SAYS as she drops into the passenger seat with a sigh. "Sorry I was a bit late. I hope we don't have reservations."

"No biggie," I reply. It actually worked out perfectly because it gave me time to finish pulling everything together for this evening.

"You look nice," she says, taking in my dark slacks and white button-down. "Does this mean I have to dress up this evening? Because I have to be honest, I was hoping that we might be able to just stay in tonight."

She cringes, and I smile on the inside.

"Really, you just want to stay home?" I ask.

"I know you were looking forward to going out, but I'm still not feeling fantastic, and I'm *so* tired. Does this make me officially old?"

"No, babe, you're not old. You're tired and getting over the flu. It's totally fine if you want to stay in."

She smiles and sighs in relief.

"You're the best."

She hasn't messed anything up for me tonight. If anything, this is better.

I pull into the driveway and hurry around the car to open the door for her. Pulling her to her feet, I walk her to the door, but then I stop her.

"Wait."

"What?" She frowns up at me.

"Let's go in through the back door."

"Why would we do that?"

"Because I mopped the floor in the living room," I lie. "And I don't know if it's dry."

"You *mopped* my hardwood?" she asks incredulously as she follows me around the house to the back door. I lead her inside and grin when I see the glow coming from the living room, but I hope she doesn't notice it yet.

"I used the wood cleaner," I assure her. We stop to say hi to the puppies, who are now blocked in the laundry room with plenty of toys and water. Angela roams around the house now, and checks on the pups throughout the day. "Let's go upstairs."

"You're very *weird* tonight," she says, but takes my offered hand and lets me lead her up the stairs. She's moving slower than she normally does. "I sure wish my hips would stop aching."

"I'm sorry you've been so sick," I say and wonder if tonight really is the right time to propose. But when she sees what I have waiting for her in the bedroom, her face brightens into curiosity, and her hand tightens in mine.

"What's this about?"

"I figured you had a long day," I reply, pleased with the flameless candles lit from the bedroom into the bathroom. There's a new robe hanging on the door, and a hot bath with her favorite bubbles already drawn for her. "Why don't you take a bit to soak and freshen up?"

"Oh, that looks so nice," she says, already stripping her scrubs over her head. "When I said you were the best, I meant you're the *best*. As in ever."

I chuckle and kiss her forehead. "Relax and get comfortable, and then meet me downstairs. Don't fall asleep. I have more surprises."

Her eyes widen. "More? Is it my birthday and I forgot?"

"No," I say with a laugh. "Just do as you're told."

I kiss her softly.

"Yes, sir," she murmurs as I leave the bathroom and hurry downstairs to get dinner in the oven and the other gifts I have for her all set up. Her house is an open concept, so keeping the stages of this process a secret isn't easy.

Just as I'm pulling the enchiladas—one of the few dishes I know how to make well—out of the oven, I hear Joy coming down the stairs, so I hurry over to greet her and lead her to the next step in my plan.

"That was decadent," she says with a smile. She's changed from her new robe into some jeans and a pretty blouse, which will be perfect. Her hair is loose around her shoulders, and her face, clean of makeup, is fresh and happy.

"Feeling better?"

"Much," she says with a nod. "And hungry. You made your enchiladas."

"I'm glad you're hungry," I say as I gesture for her to sit at the island while I dish up our plates. "I have something for you."

"Aside from the food?"

"Yes, ma'am."

She narrows her eyes at me.

"Are you trying to suck up to me for something?"

"No." I set her plate in front of her and walk around to join her. I take a bite of my food, then reach for a bag sitting on the floor by the island where she couldn't see it. "Here, open this."

"Now?"

"Now."

She smiles, chewing around a bite of food, and pulls the book out of the bag, frowning in concentration as she reads the cover.

"*Jace and Joy. Fifteen Years of Love,*" she reads, then smiles up at me. "Did you make this?"

"I did," I reply. I don't ever want to relive the hours I spent today combing through old photos of the two of us for this book. "Let's look at it."

She cracks the cover and laughs at the photo of us from our freshman year of college.

"My God, we were young," she whispers, brushing her fingertips over the photo. For the next hour, we eat dinner and look through the book, reliving the entirety of our relationship thus far. "Remember when we went on that trip to Disney our junior year?"

"How could I forget?" I ask, laughing. "You threw up after every single ride, but I couldn't get you to *not* go on them."

"You love the rides," she says as if it's as simple as that. "Of course, I rode them with you."

"Yeah, and you were miserable."

"It was worth it." She frowns, her face turning almost sad. "There are fewer photos as time goes on."

"We were both in med school and internships. Not a lot of time for photos."

"Or anything else," she adds. "Oh, that gala at the hospital for the new children's wing was fun."

"I think that was the first time you saw Will Montgomery in person."

"You're right," she says, laughing. "I was too shy to talk to him."

"I guess it all worked out in the end, now that you've met him a few times."

"Lots of things have worked out in the end. Oh, look, you even included the photo from the night of Hamilton," she says with a grin.

"Of course, you looked amazing that night."

"This is beautiful," she says after pushing her empty plate away.

"That's not the last page," I reply, feeling the butterflies start to take flight in my belly. She flips the page, then looks up at me in confusion.

"It just says: *There's more in the living room.*"

"I guess we'd better go in there, then."

She hops off her stool and follows me around the corner to the living room and gasps. I step inside the heart that I've arranged with more flameless candles and turn to her. Her eyes roam over the room, looking at the fifteen-dozen red roses—one dozen for every year I've known her—in small bouquets on the floor and on every available surface.

I extend my hand, offering it to her, and she crosses to me, stepping inside the heart with me, her jaw still dropped in surprise.

"Joy, you are the most incredible woman I've ever known. You're funny, smart, and successful and you've been my best friend since I was a boy. You've been there with me through everything, from our internships, building our careers, the death of your mother. Hell, every important moment of my life includes you, Joy. You know me better than anyone.

"You're the brightest part of my day, every day, and frankly, the idea of not having you by my side is an agony I wouldn't wish on my worst enemy. I'm standing before you now, asking you to not just be my friend, but to be my partner in all things. To have a family, to go through all of life's ups and downs, and to love with me for the rest of our lives."

There's a red velvet pillow in front of me. I kneel on one knee and pull a small box out of my pocket. I open it, offering her the ring I've had waiting just for her.

"Will you be my wife, Joy Thompson? Will you marry me?"

Tears roll down her cheeks unchecked, but she doesn't say anything. She chews her lip then, suddenly, she kneels before me, cupping my face in her hands.

"Joy? I need an answer, baby."

sixteen

Joy

He's staring at me with so much hope and love, it takes my breath away. Isn't this how every woman wants to be looked at when she's asked to marry? With adoration?

"Joy?"

"Of course," I whisper, then clear my throat and lean in to kiss him soundly. "Of course, I'll marry you, Jace Crawford."

"You scared me there," he says, tipping his forehead against mine, then reaches for the ring nestled in the box and slips it on my finger.

"This is just stunning." I tear my gaze from the solitaire diamond on my finger to Jace's face. "Thank you, so much."

"No, thank *you*." He pulls me to my feet, then lifts me in his arms and carries me upstairs. "You know what the best part of flameless candles is?"

"What's that?"

"No fire hazard." He winks at me as Carl races ahead of us up the steps. "With all of the animals in this house, I didn't dare use real candles."

"You're such a smart man." I kiss his cheek. "You know, I could get used to all these rides I get from you."

"Good. I like carrying you."

"That bath was a nice touch," I inform him as he sets me on the floor and peels the covers back on the bed. "I might have agreed to marry you from that alone. You could have proposed when I was sitting in that water, and I would have scrambled to say yes."

"Good to know the way to your heart is through the tub," he says, his eyes full of humor.

"Should we make some calls?" I ask. "Noel will freak if she's not the first to know."

"She already knows," he says with a laugh. "Sometimes, a guy needs a little help."

"You asked her to help you?" I don't know why, but that touches me. That they worked together to make this proposal special means a lot to me. "That's sweet."

"I wanted to make sure that tonight was romantic and exactly what you'd want."

"And you did," I reply, just before he lowers his lips to mine, kissing me with love and passion. He steps closer, pressing himself against me, and I can feel his hardness against my belly. "I guess it's been a few days."

"Too long," he agrees. "But you've been sick."

"I'm feeling better now." I wiggle my brows and laugh when he tackles me to the bed, his face buried in my neck. He immediately unfastens my jeans and dives inside with a hand, finding me wet and wanting.

"You're slick," he says. His movements gentle, and he

unwraps me from my clothes like I'm the best present ever. "And so fucking beautiful."

"You're not so bad yourself," I inform him as I slide my hand up under the hem of his shirt and over the rigid muscles of his abs. "Seriously, your stomach should come with a warning label."

He grins against my left breast before taking the nipple into his mouth and sucking gently.

"What would it say?" he asks.

"May cause spontaneous horniness," I reply with a laugh as he strips out of his shirt and tosses it aside.

"This stomach?" He flexes his muscles, making me laugh harder.

"Yes, those muscles. Don't get a big head, now."

"The woman I love just agreed to marry me," he says, falling over me again and kissing me deeply. "My head is huge."

"You're silly."

"You're beautiful," he breathes and kisses his way down my sternum to my belly, before covering me with his body once again and filling me up. "You're incredible, Joy."

He's moving, in and out in a steady rhythm, not too slow and not too fast. My toes curl, and my fingers fist in his hair, holding on tightly as I feel an orgasm already making its way down my spine.

"God, the way you make me feel," he whispers in my ear, and it sends me over into a silent, intense climax that leaves me reeling and loving him more—something I didn't even think was possible.

Once we're cleaned up and snuggling in bed, Jace clears his throat.

"How long should this engagement be, do you think?"

"I don't know." I frown up at him. "Are you in a hurry?"

"Well, yeah. I'm anxious to make you Dr. Crawford."

I slowly shake my head. "I'm still going to be Dr. Thompson."

"Like hell."

"No, really, Jace, I won't be changing my last name."

"What are you talking about?" He scowls down at me. "We're getting married, and we were both raised with traditional family values. Of course, you'll change your name."

"It's not about that." I sigh and rub my hands over my face, trying to gather my thoughts. "Jace, my entire business is under my name as Dr. Joy Thompson. That's how my patients know me, but more than that, it's how everything is filed with the IRS. Dismantling it all and putting it back together will take months, if not *years*."

"People do it every day." His expression is hard.

"I'm not trying to hurt you," I insist. "This isn't because I don't love you, or that I'm not proud of you. You know that."

"I just don't understand," he replies.

"Can we talk it out another time?" I ask wearily. "This is all so new, and we should be excited not bickering like an old couple."

"Okay." He sighs and tugs me closer. "We'll talk about it later."

"I DON'T WANT a red car," I insist the next day. We're at the dealership, looking for a new vehicle to replace the one that died the other day. "And I think I want an SUV."

"Okay," Jace says with a nod, and we walk toward a line of

mid-sized SUVs on the car lot. We haven't been approached by a salesman yet, but it's only a matter of time. "What color *do* you like?"

"Silver or black. And it doesn't need a sunroof. I'd never use it anyway."

"Joy, you can have any car you want. If you don't want to decide today, we can do some research so you can narrow it down to what you really want."

I blow out a gusty breath. "I hate buying cars."

"I know." He kisses my forehead. "We can leave if you want."

"No, I need a car. I like that black one there," I say, pointing to the SUV straight ahead. Just as we reach it, a salesman approaches and tells me all of the reasons why I should want a vehicle with more bells and whistles.

"Look," I interrupt. "I appreciate that you have to sell cars. It's your job. But I'm telling you I like *this* one. It suits my needs just fine, and I don't need or want anything fancier."

The guy looks at Jace, which irritates the hell out of me.

"And no, I don't need to ask his permission to make this decision."

Jace presses his lips together, trying horribly to keep his laughter at bay. He's been with me to buy cars before.

He knows how much I loathe it.

Which is why I don't do it often.

"That's fine with me," Randy, the salesman, says. "Do you want to test drive this one?"

"Yes," I reply and spend the next fifteen minutes driving literally around the block before pulling back into the lot. "I'll take it."

"That was fast," he says.

"I make decisions quickly, and I hate to shop." I hop out of the SUV, not missing the shrug of apology from Jace. He thinks this is hilarious. All I can think is, *this is a Sunday of my life that I'll never get back.*

Once we're at Randy's desk, he punches up numbers, offers me extra warranties and other things that I pass on, and when it comes time to pay for it, Jace shocks the shit out of me by telling Randy he'll be paying for it.

"Like hell you are," I say, looking at Jace like he's grown a new head. "This is my car."

"Give us a moment, please?" Jace says calmly without looking away from my face. Randy nods and leaves, after telling us to take all the time we need. "I'm about to be your husband, and I can afford to buy you this car."

"I don't *need* you to buy me this car," I reply. "Yes, you're going to be my husband, but that doesn't mean you pay for everything."

"You do realize that you're arguing with someone willing to pay cash for a brand-new car for you."

"Yeah, because it's not necessary. Thank you for the offer, but I'm fine. I've got this."

His eyes narrow, and I take his hands in mine. "Look, I know you want to feel like you're taking care of me, and I love you so much for it. But this isn't the way to do that. You take care of me in little ways every day. I don't need you for financial things, but it's really good to know that I have you if I should need you."

He sighs, still looking in my eyes and nods. "I don't agree, but okay. I apologize for assuming."

"No need." I kiss his cheek. "You can assume all you want. I'll let you know when I have a difference of opinion. Now, let's get this over with."

⌒

"YOU'VE CLEANED THAT sink three times," I inform him later Sunday night. The shiny new SUV is sitting in my driveway, and we've been home for a couple of hours, but Jace hasn't sat down once. He's been cleaning my house like a crazy man.

"I have nervous energy," he says.

"You don't say." I gently take the sponge from him. "Jace, you're about to take the finish off the surface."

"I can fold laundry."

Before he can step away, I catch his hand in mine and pull him to me.

"Talk to me."

"I have the meeting with the attorneys tomorrow morning."

"I know, and they're going to tell you that all is well."

"I hope you're right."

"Jace, don't stress this. It's going to be fine. *You're* going to be fine."

"I need them to tell me I can go back to work." He rests his forehead against mine. "I *need* it."

"I know. It's not gotten easier with time for you."

"It's worse," he admits. "I love being with you, but—"

"But you're a surgeon," I finish for him and smile at the relief in his eyes. "I have a great feeling about tomorrow. And taking all of this aggression out on my house isn't making it better. I don't think it's ever been this clean."

"And you're complaining?"

"Well, I think I lost some paint off of that wall you scrubbed for twenty minutes."

"No paint was lost," he says, wrapping his arms low around my back. "Besides, I know someone who knows her way around a paintbrush."

"Really? Who would that be?"

"She's gorgeous. And smart."

"Hmm . . . Do I know her?"

He bites my neck, sending shivers down my spine.

"You know her intimately."

"Well, she sounds like a heck of a woman."

"She's the love of my life."

seventeen

Jace

"We've settled," Howard, one of three attorneys says the following morning. The three of them, along with Mick, my medical director, all have smiles on their faces, obviously satisfied with the outcome of the case. "You're free to come back to work anytime."

"Today, preferably," Mick interjects. "Your office is waiting for you. I'd like for you to get caught up on some paperwork today, and get back into surgery tomorrow."

I blow out a breath and lean back in my chair, staring at them in surprise. This is the news I wanted to hear.

"Are you okay, Jace?" Howard asks.

"I think I'm so relieved that I don't know what to say," I admit with a grin. "What did they settle on?"

"One-point-two million dollars," Howard says. "And they agreed to sign documents stating that you were not at fault."

"Fuck," I mutter, shaking my head. "That's a shit ton of money."

"Well spent," Mick says. "This is the best outcome for the hospital and our patients, Jace. We need you, and if we'd not pursued a settlement, it could have dragged on for years in the courts. At the end of the day, we all get what we want."

"I hope they signed an NDA, so they can't run to the press, and in doing so encourage everyone to file suits when they lose a family member."

"Of course," Howard says with a nod. "It's all been taken care of. Your name can't be mentioned, and they can't come back to ask for more money. We all move on with our lives."

I blow out a gusty breath and stand, then shake each of their hands. "I'd better get to my office."

"Happy to have you back, Jace," Mick says with a nod.

I hurry down to my office, shut the door, and take a deep breath. At least Sean Tiller, the doctor from Boston that I don't like, didn't leave a mess behind, thankfully.

Or he did, and it was cleaned up before today.

The words on the door say, *Jace Crawford, M.D. Chief of Surgery*.

"I'm back," I whisper, then rub my hands together and reach for my phone, calling Joy first and foremost. "Hi, Susan, this is Jace. May I please speak with Joy?"

"Yes, I've been given instructions to interrupt her when you call. Hold, please."

I grin, staring out the window at the Seattle skyline as I wait for Joy. In less than thirty seconds, she picks up the phone. "Hey! Tell me the good news."

"You were right," I reply and quickly give her a rundown of the meeting. "So, I'm in my office, getting caught up on what is most likely a paperwork pile the size of Mount Everest."

"I'm *so* happy for you, Jace," she says, a smile in her voice. "Congratulations."

"Thanks. Hey, why don't you come by the hospital at around

six and we'll have dinner in the cafeteria?"

"I love their food," she says. "It's a date. Have a good day."

It's not a good day, it's a fucking fantastic day. Despite the number of emails to read and amount of paperwork to get through, the morning and afternoon fly by. Nurses and other physicians drop in to welcome me back.

I'm finally back where I need to be.

At six o'clock sharp, there's a knock on my door.

"Come in," I call, not looking up from my computer.

"You look hot sitting at that desk, Dr. Crawford."

I grin as Joy saunters across my office, still dressed in her own scrubs. Rather than sitting across from me, she walks around the desk and sits in my lap.

"I came straight here."

"I'm glad." I bury my face in the crook of her neck and take a deep breath. "I need the break, and it's *so* good to see you."

"They already have you slaving away," she says softly, running her fingers through my hair. I can feel the muscles in my neck and shoulders begin to relax.

"I don't mind," I reply honestly.

"Are you hungry?"

"Famished," I admit as she steps off my lap and leads me out of the office. I lock the door behind me and escort her to the elevators.

At this time of day, the cafeteria shouldn't be too busy because most of the daytime staff has gone home, and the evening staff has just arrived. Breakfast and lunch are chaotic.

"I want the taco salad," Joy says as we approach the line. "They have the *best* taco salads."

"That sounds good," I agree with a nod and have the same thing. We load our trays with the salads, drinks, and a dessert to share, and find a table in the back corner to eat and talk.

"So delicious," Joy says around a big bite. "I'll come have dinner with you more often."

"I hope so. How was your day?"

"Not bad, actually. It was a lighter day. No surgeries, so that was good. Dad's at my place with the puppies."

"They're not going to stay in the laundry room for long."

"I know," she says with a shrug. "They'll be ready for new homes in a couple of weeks. I can't believe how fast the time has gone."

"It'll be easier for you when they find homes." I reach out and give her hand a squeeze.

"Angela will be happier, too," she says with a laugh. "The pups are at the age where they just annoy her more than anything."

"Dr. Crawford?" Peter Kratz, one of my colleagues, interrupts our dinner to chat about a lung transplant he's performing tomorrow on a cystic fibrosis patient. After twenty minutes, I agree to scrub in for as long as I can and assist. This is a special, fragile case that he's more than qualified to do, but he'd like to have all hands on deck. "Thank you, see you tomorrow. Good to have you back."

"Have a good night," I reply with a nod and look over to find Joy frowning. "What's wrong?"

"This is going to sound stupidly selfish."

"Shoot."

She sighs. "I'm *so* happy for you, and proud that you're back to work doing what you love."

"But?"

"But it also sucks because I'll never see you." The last few words are whispered. "And I'm going to miss you."

"That's not true," I insist, taking her hand in mine again. "Joy, *you're* my priority, always. I know we didn't see each other in the past, but we had a different dynamic then."

"I don't see how it can be different now," she says. "You'll still be both the chief *and* a surgeon, and both of those are full-time jobs."

"I'm going to make it work," I insist. "I can make all of it work. You'll see."

She smiles, but it doesn't reach her eyes, and I'm more determined than ever to prove to her that she will *not* take a back seat to my career.

TWO WEEKS AND one day.

That's how long it's been since I last saw her face.

Touched her skin.

I'm failing.

I rush to my office and check my phone. It's after midnight, and I missed three texts and a call from Joy.

"Shit," I mutter. God, I'm tired. Bone-tired, and I miss her something fierce.

So rather than call her back, I make a snap decision to go to her house. I've been staying at my place because it's closer to the hospital, and I've been working twenty-hour days. Some nights, I don't even bother to go home, using the couch in my office as a place to nap before starting work again early the next morning.

It's a pace that just a few years ago I would have thrived on.

Now, I'm just plain exhausted.

I pull into Joy's driveway and let myself into the house. It's dark and quiet since Joy would have gone to bed a couple of hours ago.

It sounds like she's been working a lot, too. At least, that's what I've gathered from her texts.

I climb the stairs and scratch Angela behind the ears when she meets me at the door of Joy's bedroom.

"Good girl," I whisper in her ear. "Are you watching over her for me?"

Angela just licks my cheek then returns to her bed at the foot of Joy's.

That's new.

I shuck out of my clothes and slide between the covers, scooting up to Joy and pulling her into my arms.

"Jace?" she whispers.

"If it's someone else, we need to have a conversation," I reply with a smile and kiss her firmly, pressing her against me. "I'm so sorry, baby."

"It is what it is," she says with a sigh, and I hate the disappointment in her voice. I don't want to let her down. I just need to get settled at work, and then I can shift my focus to Joy.

It shouldn't take long to get caught up.

A tiny voice whispers *"liar"* in the back of my head, but I ignore it and tuck her under me, sinking into her for the first time in weeks.

She's everything good in my world.

She's home.

Dear Jace, this is your long-lost fiancée, Joy. I haven't had a conversation with you in weeks. Call me.

I smile at the text from Joy and sigh. It's been a week since I slipped into her bed and made love to her. I just couldn't stay away another moment.

Time is flying. Every minute of my day is full of surgery, questions, issues to resolve, and battles to settle. Sometimes, I feel like a babysitter.

But it's important, and I love it.

Just not as much as I love Joy.

"You look deep in thought."

I glance up to find Maria Sanchez standing in my doorway. She's in her white coat and dark slacks, a stethoscope around her neck, her lips painted that signature deep red she favors.

She's a beautiful woman, and once upon a time, we had a lot of fun together.

Those days are over.

"I'm busy," I reply, but can't send her away because I'm her boss now. "What can I do for you?"

Her eyes roam up and down my body, setting me on edge. Looks like that weren't appropriate before I was her boss, but I was single, and she's beautiful.

They're beyond out of line now.

"Well, aside from the obvious, I need to discuss my surgery schedule next week."

"Come in," I reply with a sigh, tucking my phone away and making a mental note to call Joy as soon as Maria leaves my office.

"I need to ask someone to cover for me next Thursday and Friday," she begins. "I have travel plans."

"Then you should have had the days covered weeks ago," I reply with a frown. "I don't know who will pick it up for you on this short notice."

"Someone will," she says with a shrug. "Either way, I won't be here."

I blow out a breath, trying to keep my irritation under control. Has this always been Maria's work ethic?

If so, I wouldn't have known. She's an orthopedic surgeon, so I never would have been asked to cover for her.

I make a mental note to ask Mick about it later.

"If we can't find someone to take your surgeries, you'll have to stay."

She scowls. "No, if no one takes them, we will reschedule them. This isn't *heart* surgery, no one will die if they have to wait a week."

"Maria, some of the people on your schedule have been there for months. You can't just move them around because you want to go away for the weekend. They have schedules and lives, too."

"Well, I'm the one doing the surgery, so I make the rules."

"Actually, no. *I* make the rules, and I'm telling you that if I can't find a replacement for those days, and you don't show up, you'll be fired."

Her eyes flare with temper. "I'll sue you so fast your head will spin."

"Do it," I challenge her. "The policy is written in your contract."

She presses her lips together, knowing that she's been out-smarted. She narrows her eyes. "So, how's your *girlfriend*?"

"My fiancée is fine, thank you."

This makes her tilt her head in surprise. She watches me with calculation.

"Jace, this is silly." She stands and paces my office, then walks to where I'm sitting behind my desk and drags her fingers along my shoulders, making my skin crawl. "You know we can work this out. I'll do just about *anything* to have those days off."

"Surely, you're not implying that I would give you the time off in exchange for fucking you."

Her brown eyes turn cold. "Why not?"

I grab her hand and push it away from me. "I didn't give you permission to touch me. I told you before, this isn't going to happen. If you touch me again or make another offer like the one you just did, I'll file a sexual harassment suit."

She snorts out a laugh. "Oh, that's rich. Who's going to believe that *I'm* the one harassing *you*? Maybe you raped me."

"You're fired," Mick says from the doorway of my office, his nostrils flaring with rage. "Get your shit and get the fuck out of my hospital."

"Dr. Leamon," she says, blinking rapidly and shaking her head. "You misunderstood, Jace and I were just joking around."

"I heard the whole conversation," he says. "And threatening the chief of surgery is grounds for dismissal. No second chances."

"I *need* this job."

"You should have thought of that before." He dismisses her with a flick of the wrist. "Now leave, before I have you removed."

She stomps out of my office and slams the door behind

her. I sigh deeply.

"If you fuck another doctor on staff, you'll be fired, as well," he says.

I cringe. "It was before I was chief. Way before. She wouldn't let it go."

"I'm not kidding," he says.

"I'm engaged, and happily, it's not with another physician on staff," I inform him.

"That's concerning, as well," he replies. "We talked about this when you were appointed chief."

"I know. And I'll make it work."

He narrows his eyes at me.

"*You're* married," I remind him.

"And it was a miracle that I didn't get divorced," he retorts. "It's a miracle she didn't throw me out on my ass. I was *never* home, Jace. For years. You sacrifice a lot for this job."

"I can make it work," I insist again. "I'm not saying it'll be easy, but it'll be worth it."

He's quiet for a moment, watching me through his glasses. "I'll be checking in with you to make sure you're not burning out."

I'm already burning out.

But I just smile and nod. "So noted. What did you come in here for?" I ask before he can walk out the door.

"Just checking in, and I'm glad I did. Now we need to get to work finding a new orthopedic surgeon."

"Great," I mutter after he leaves. "One more thing to do."

I pick up my phone and dial Joy's number, but it goes to voicemail.

"Hey, baby," I say into the phone. "I know I've been bad at

communication this week. And, well, every week. I was just thinking about you and wanted to say hi. I hope you're having a good day. Love you."

I hang up and sigh.

I miss her.

eighteen

Joy

"I can't even wear my engagement ring," I say to my doctor. "My fingers are too swollen. I've been nauseated off and on for more than a *month*."

"And you're just now coming to see me?" she asks with a scowl.

"The flu has made the rounds through my clinic, and I assume I'm still getting over that."

"Not a month later," she says, shaking her head. "Are you dizzy?"

"No."

"Diarrhea?"

"Thankfully, no. I am achy. Especially in my hips."

She looks up at me and narrows her eyes. "First things first, I'm going to have you pee in a cup. We'll take a look at things, and then if I think we need a blood test, we'll do that. I have a hunch on something."

"On what?"

"Just pee in the cup, and I'll be back in a few. The bathroom is around the corner."

She takes her laptop out of the room, points at the bathroom, and leaves me to my own devices.

I finally had to break down and come to the doctor. My hips are *killing* me. I can't lay on my back at all anymore, and I am constantly shifting in my sleep, trying to find a comfortable position.

The nausea comes in waves now. Some days, I'm completely fine. Other days, I can't keep anything down.

It's ridiculously frustrating.

I do my business, write my name on the cup, and put it in the mysterious two-sided door, then wash my hands and return to the exam room.

Less than ten minutes later, Dr. Nixon returns with a smile on her pretty face.

"It's just as I suspected."

"I have malaria."

She laughs and shakes her head. "No, you're pregnant."

I blink at her, sure I've misheard her.

"I have the flu?"

"Pregnant," she repeats, enunciating each syllable. "You, my friend, are going to have a baby."

I squint my eyes at her, blinking as if I don't understand the words coming out of her mouth. "A baby."

"A baby," she confirms with a nod. "Now, let's do an ultrasound and find out how far along you are."

"An ultrasound."

"Are you just going to repeat everything I say?"

I nod slowly. "Yeah, I think I am because I am *not* having a baby."

"Your pregnancy test was positive," she says gently. "I take it you've not been trying to get pregnant."

"Well, now that I think about it, I haven't been trying *not* to get pregnant. We were great about protection in the beginning and then it just sort of fizzled out. I'm a horrible person."

"Is he in the picture for the long haul?"

I hold up my hand, then remember that I can't wear my ring right now because of my fat sausage fingers. "Yes. He proposed a month ago."

"Well, congratulations," she says as her nurse rolls an ultrasound machine into the room. I remove my pants, not shy enough to need them to leave the room, and lie back on the table, my feet in the stirrups.

This is a vaginal ultrasound, so it's not particularly comfortable, but with some maneuvering, Dr. Nixon smiles and points to a black blob on the screen. "There it is."

"It's tiny."

"I'd say you're about eight weeks along."

I frown. "We were still using condoms then."

"They don't always work," she says with a shrug. "I see more than my share of women who swear they used condoms."

"Well, that feels like false advertising on the condoms' behalf," I reply, my eyes glued to the screen. "Is that . . . ?"

"Yep, that's a heartbeat." She pushes buttons and moves the wand again. The blip moves in and out of sight, but the heartbeat is strong and steady. "It looks to me like things are healthy, and right where they should be. You'll need to make an appointment with your OB, of course."

"Of course," I mutter, still shocked. The doctor removes the wand and backs away.

"You can get dressed. I can prescribe some anti-nausea meds for you for the bad days, but this should pass in another month or so."

"Thanks," I reply.

"Let me know if you need anything. Congrats again."

She pats my shoulder, and then she's gone. I clean myself up and get dressed, check out at the front desk, and hurry out to my car where I sit and stare at the cars driving back and forth on the road in front of me.

I'm going to have a baby.

Holy shit.

My first reaction is happiness. A baby is something to be excited about. But I also feel nervous and worried.

I have reservations about Jace. Are we even getting married at this point? I haven't seen him since the night he slipped into my bed. He left before I woke up the next morning. I've received exactly one call and three texts since then.

It's been a month since he went back to work. I knew he'd be busy. I *knew.*

But I also believed him when he said he'd make me a priority.

So, I don't know what's going to happen, and it makes my heart ache.

I reach for my phone and dial Jace, hoping that a miracle will happen and he'll answer. I know one thing for sure, I have to talk to him.

"Hey," he says, his smooth voice coming through the phone.

"Wow, I caught you."

"I know. I'm sorry, Joy."

All he does is apologize these days.

"I'd really love to see you," I say, unable to hide the

desperation in my voice. "Jace, I haven't seen you in weeks."

"You have impeccable timing," he says. "I'm getting out of here by four. Let's have dinner. I'll pick you up and take you to the Palomino."

"That actually sounds really good," I reply, relief pouring through me. We can have dinner at our favorite place, and I can tell him about the baby.

"Great, I'll come to your place at five. That'll give me time to swing by home and clean up."

"Perfect. I'll see you soon. And, Jace, if you stand me up, so help me God—"

"I won't," he assures me. "I'm going to see you in exactly two hours and thirty-four minutes."

"Okay. Love you."

"I love you, too, sweetheart."

I hang up and drive home, hope blooming in my heart for the first time in a while. I don't even feel sick to my stomach, which is a blessing in and of itself.

Everything is going to be okay. This baby isn't a horrible thing. Jace told me when he proposed that he wants a family, and we're both established in our careers, at the perfect time to add a little human.

We're going to make it work.

The house is quiet when I walk inside. It's been particularly quiet since I found all six of Angela's puppies new homes. It wasn't easy to say goodbye, but they each have wonderful families to love them. And, I think Angela is relieved, too.

She greets me at the door, whining with happiness to see me.

"Hi, special girl." I kiss the top of her snout. "Jace is coming to get me soon. You have to come help me decide what to wear.

That's right, come on."

We climb the stairs to my bedroom, and I open the closet. I want to look nice. Scratch that. I want to blow him the fuck away.

Remind him what he's been missing out on.

With a decisive nod, I pull a shift dress out that will look great with a belt. It has long sleeves, appropriate for the fall weather, but if I leave a button undone, I can show off a little cleavage.

Perfect.

After taking the time to relax in a bath, wash my hair, and then buff and polish myself into something that resembles sexy, it's five-oh-five, and Jace isn't here.

I scowl at the time on my phone, and it coincidentally rings. "Hello."

"Babe, I'm *so* sorry. I'm not cancelling, I just got hung up on an emergency. Go ahead and go to the restaurant. I'll meet you there."

"*Jace.*"

"I swear, I'll meet you there in just a little while. Get a glass of wine and save me a seat. I'll see you soon, and I'll make it up to you."

"Trust me, you'll be making it up to me."

"In spades," he promises. "See you soon."

I blow out a breath and look over at Carl, who stares at me with narrowed eyes.

"I know, he's in trouble."

He continues staring at me.

"Stop judging me. He'll make it up to me."

I grab my handbag and keys and leave for the restaurant.

I'm a good thirty minutes away with traffic, and once I park and walk inside, it's almost an hour after I left my house.

Surely, he'll be right behind me.

"MORE SPARKLING WATER?" the waiter asks me two hours later. I'm in the middle of eating my steak and potatoes. I finally decided to go ahead and order some food since I was here and starving.

But Jace hasn't shown.

"Please," I say with a nod.

"Dr. Thompson?"

I glance up and smile at Alec, the owner of the sock-eating Great Dane.

"Hi, Alec."

"I thought that was you. Are you waiting for someone, or can I sit and chat for a minute?"

"Please," I say, gesturing to Jace's empty seat, burying my fury so I don't take it out on an innocent bystander. "What are you up to?"

"I'm here with my parents and sister, celebrating my dad's birthday, but I saw you sitting here on my way back from the restroom. Do you come here by yourself often?"

"No, actually. I was supposed to meet someone, but they got hung up, and I was hungry."

"I see." He nods. "Well, you look lovely."

"Thank you." I smile, enjoying the company and the compliment. "So do you."

Alec is a handsome man, with jet-black hair, brown eyes,

and an athletic body. He's tall, and he's always been kind to me.

"How is the dog?" I ask and take a bite of my steak.

"She's good," he replies with a chuckle. "She's stopped eating socks and is slowly starting to calm down a bit."

"I'm glad. I think she'll be a great dog once she outgrows her puppyhood."

"You're right. And the kids adore her."

"Are they with you tonight?"

A shadow drifts over his face. "No. Their mom wouldn't let me bring them tonight because it's not my scheduled time with them."

"Divorce sucks," I say with a cringe, and I inwardly hope against hope that this won't be Jace and me someday, fighting over custody and when each of us gets to see our child. "It's not getting any better with time?"

"No," he says, shaking his head. "And it doesn't help that she started dating someone else. I think she thinks that she and this new guy can pick up where our family left off, and just squeeze me right out of the picture."

"Oh, Alec, I'm sure that's not the case."

"Feels that way," he says with a sigh.

"This new guy is shiny and new," I reply reasonably. "Of course, she's preoccupied with him. But she shouldn't try to use him as an excuse for you to not see your children."

"It's something different all the time," he says. *"Tim wants to take us to Portland for the weekend. Tim wants to take us all to the movies. Tim this and Tim that."*

Alec rolls his eyes.

"You might have to call your lawyer," I suggest. "I know it's expensive and no one likes going that route, but you have the right to be with your kids."

"I've already made the call," he says. "You know, I never would have thought we'd be here. We were as in love as anyone, with a happy family. A nice home. Good careers. And then, out of the blue, *bam*. She's unhappy and wants out. Just like that. No explanation. Just wants out."

"I'm sorry."

He shakes his head. "No, I'm sorry. I've just taken up a good portion of your evening bitching about my ex-wife."

"Well, I wasn't doing anything else, and you helped take my mind off of my own problems."

"What's going on with you?"

I sigh, wondering where to begin. I can't tell him about the baby. I haven't even told my family about that yet.

Hell, I haven't even told *Jace*.

"Let's just say that relationships are complicated."

"I hear you," he says with a nod. "You know, we were just wrapping up dinner. I'd love to take you out for dessert."

Before I can reply, I hear, "She won't be going anywhere with you."

My head whips around, and I find a very angry Jace standing behind me.

"Looks like your friend is here," Alec says and winks at me before nodding at Jace and respectfully walking away.

Alec is a good guy. If I weren't ridiculously in love with Jace, I'd consider dating him.

"Hello," I say as Jace takes his seat and glares at me from across the table. I open the check that I've already paid, put my card away, and sign the credit card slip, all without saying another word to the man sitting across from me.

"That's it?" he asks.

"That's it," I confirm as I drink the last of my water.

"Where is your engagement ring?" His lips are tight, his eyes shooting daggers, and I want to laugh. Maybe it's hormones, but I don't want to cry or rage at him. I don't want to slap him as much as I did just minutes ago.

No, I want to laugh my ass off from the sheer absurdity of it all.

"It's at home," I reply, not taking my eyes off of his. I'm practically *daring* him to start something here in this restaurant.

"Were you planning on breaking up with me tonight?" he asks, and all I can do is roll my eyes.

Jesus, I don't need this from him. I don't need the jealousy, his insecurity.

If anyone should be feeling insecure here, it's *me*.

So, I do the adult thing, and rather than start a big knock-down, drag-out here in my favorite restaurant, I grab my purse, stand, and walk out of the building.

nineteen

Joy

"**Y**ou've lost your damn mind," I mutter to myself as I march out of the building, my shoes clicking smartly on the sidewalk.

"Joy," Jace barks behind me. "Stop right now and tell me what the *fuck* is going on."

"No." I stop and round on him, fire consuming me. "You don't get to talk to me like that. You don't get to be mad, Jace. You're almost *three goddamn hours* late! What did you expect me to do?"

"Well, I didn't expect you to find a new date, I'll tell you that right now."

"Jesus," I mutter, turning away in disgust. "He's a client from work who saw me there *alone* and stopped to chat."

"And invite you out to *dessert*," he snarls, wrinkling his nose at *dessert*. "Would you rather go with him, Joy?"

"No," I reply honestly. "No, I'd rather my fiancé show up when he says he will. But I *should* want to go with him. I shouldn't stand here and give you the chance to explain yourself.

I haven't seen you in a *month*. And no, sneaking into my bed in the middle of the night to get your rocks off doesn't count."

He snarls, truly irate at me for the first time in the fifteen years I've known him.

"You *knew* that I'd be swamped at work."

"Yep," I reply with a nod. "I did. And I told you that. And then you *swore* to me that I wouldn't feel less than your job. That you'd make me a priority. You've never broken a promise to me before this."

"Joy, I'm trying to get my feet under me."

"Yeah? Me, too!"

"You—"

"I'm pregnant," I interrupt and watch his eyes go wide as we stand in silence staring at each other, our breaths coming fast in the cool night.

"What did you say?"

"I'm pregnant," I repeat, softer this time.

"How long have you known?"

I narrow my eyes at him. "About six hours, Jace. But if I'd known for *six days*, you still wouldn't know because you don't return a fucking phone call."

"Can we get past the fact that I'm a fuck-up in the communication department and go back to the whole pregnancy thing?"

"Sure." I cross my arms over my chest. I don't love that we're having this conversation on the sidewalk, but I'll be damned if I invite him back to my house. "The nausea, the swelling, aches? Not the flu. I'm knocked up."

"You said it wasn't the right time to get pregnant."

I narrow my eyes at him again. Okay, *now* I want to slap him. "It wasn't. Obviously, it's not an exact science. You should know that, *Dr.* Crawford."

"All right." He holds up his hands in surrender and shakes his head. "This is ridiculous. I'm not blaming you for anything, and this is a great thing."

"Is it?" I demand, cocking my head to the side. "Really? Because I'm not so sure."

"What are you talking about?"

"I'm not sure about *anything.* I don't know if I want to marry you, Jace. What kind of a father and husband will you be? The kind who's never around? Who misses birthdays and holidays and soccer games because someone is dying somewhere and *you're* the only doctor who can fix them? You're not *here.*"

It's obvious he's fuming, his hands curl into fists at his sides as he stands and silently listens to me rant.

"Maybe this schedule was okay when you were my best friend, and I had my own life, and I was just so fucking *proud* of you. I still am!" I throw my hands in the air and pace around the sidewalk. "But it's not okay now. We're not just friends, and I'm too needy. We knew that sleeping together would change everything, and it did. I'm in love with you. I'm not willing to accept the scraps you throw me when the job has finished chewing you up and spitting you out."

"That's not fair."

"No." I shrug, shaking my head. "No, it's not fair at all. And yet, here we are. You're so fucking stubborn, you think you can make it all fall into place and work out, but Jace, you *can't.* You're one man, and there are only twenty-four hours in a day."

"What do you want me to do?" he demands. "Do you want me to quit being a surgeon?"

"No. You *are* a surgeon. It's your lifeblood." I want to go to him, to wrap my arms around him and assure us both that it'll all be okay.

But I'm not convinced that it will be.

"I don't want to lose you," he says and swallows hard.

"I don't want that, either. I don't know what the answer is, but I know what it *isn't*. This past month has been hell for me, Jace. I completely lost you, and I will not do that to our child. We need you. So, I suggest you get it together and figure out how you're going to be there for us because we deserve nothing less than that."

I lay my hand over my still-flat stomach, and his eyes follow the motion, softening with love.

"I love you, Joy."

"I love you, too."

Tears threaten as I gaze at him, and then I can't take it anymore. I turn away and march down the sidewalk to my car. Once inside, I fire the engine and drive away, desperate to put some miles between us. I don't want him to see me fall apart.

Not like this.

And I can't crumble in the way I need to because I can't endanger the baby. So, I point my car in the direction of Noel's house.

I need her.

I'm ringing the bell incessantly when she finally comes to the door. Her eyes widen when she sees my face.

"What's wrong?"

"I just—" I shake my head, the tears coming freely now. "I just needed someone."

"Come on." She wraps her arm around my shoulders and leads me into the house. "Are you hurt?"

"Just my heart," I blurt out as we sit on the couch. I curl up in the corner and let the floodgates open, crying like I never have before.

"I'm going to kill him," she says, her voice full of anger and righteousness. "I swear to God, he's a dead man."

I shake my head and fall into her lap, letting her play with my hair as I sob all of the disappointment, fear, and worry away.

It's been a long day and an even longer month.

When the tears slow, she passes me a fresh Kleenex, and I sit up, wiping my eyes and coming away with a black tissue.

"Ruined my makeup," I sniff.

"And how," she agrees. "Wanna talk about it?"

"Yeah. I'm going to have a baby."

"Holy shit!" She pulls me to her, hugging me fiercely. "Is this why you're upset? Oh my God, did Jace ditch you when he found out?"

"No." I laugh despite myself. "No, he wouldn't do that. But I told him that he needs to get his shit together."

"Good advice," she says with a thoughtful nod. "But you need to tell me everything. From the beginning."

I take a deep breath. "Well, they settled the lawsuit . . ."

"HAND ME THAT screwdriver," Dad says, pointing to my left. I needed to come and talk to him. I went to bed late last night without even one word from Jace.

"This one?"

"Yeah."

I pass it over and sigh as Dad dives back under his truck,

tinkering away. Nancy is sleeping on a blanket next to the front tire. She's never far away from my dad, and it makes my heart happy.

They love each other.

"What brings you over? Not that I'm not happy to see you, I'm just surprised," he says, and I bite my lip.

Maybe telling him I'm knocked up when I can't see his face is a good thing.

Suck it up, buttercup.

"Can you come out from under there?"

He slides out, wiping his hands on a towel and stands, watching me with eyes the same color as mine.

"What's up? Are you okay?"

"Oh, yeah." I swallow and nod. "Yeah, I'm fine. I just wanted to come by and tell you that you're going to be a grandpa."

Dad's eyes light up, and he wraps me in his arms, spinning me around the garage.

"Well, this is great news. Where's Jace?" He glances out the door toward my car, but I shake my head.

"I'm not sure."

He frowns. "Well, is he excited?"

"I don't know that either," I admit with a deep breath, taking in the musty smell of motor oil and garage. "We had a fight last night when I told him."

"A fight?" He frowns and leads me into the house, then puts the kettle on for some tea. "What on earth did you fight about?"

"I haven't seen him, Dad." I sit at the kitchen table and rub my hands over my face. My eyes are still tender from crying on Noel last night. "Since he went back to work last month, I've barely seen him."

"And?"

I uncover my face and stare at him as if he didn't hear me.

"We're engaged, and I haven't seen him," I repeat, but he shrugs as he waits for the water to boil.

"You've known that Jace works a lot of hours. He always has."

"I know." I nod and trace the wood grain in the table. "But he promised that he'd make more time for me now that things have changed between us, and if anything, it's worse."

"Because he's been catching up from being gone from the hospital for a month, and he's still getting used to a new position of authority." He nods, thinking it over. "Don't you think you're being a bit selfish?"

"*Selfish?*" I scowl, my hackles up. "Dad, I don't think it's selfish to want to spend time with my fiancé."

"Not at all," he agrees. "That's not the selfish part."

"What kind of a father is he going to be?" I blurt out, making him frown. "I know he'll love us, but it's his *time* we need. His fancy car, and house, and all the rest of it? I don't care, Dad. We need *him*."

"So, you want him to show up as a father, but in the past month, have you shown up as a *partner?*"

"Well, I've called and texted. I got no answer."

"Did you go up to that hospital and take him lunch? Stop by in the evening with a fresh pair of clothes and a hug to encourage him?"

"He's *working*."

"And I know Jace," he interrupts. "He would take the fifteen minutes to see you and be grateful that you thought of him."

"No," I say with a loud exhale, feeling defeated. "I didn't do those things. I wallowed in self-pity."

"Relationships are all about compromise, Joy. It's not all about *you*. You had a month with him when he had nothing else to do with his time but devote every minute of the day to you, but that's not who he is."

"No," I murmur, shame washing through me. "It's not."

"And you can't expect him to dive back into the deep end and not give him some slack to get it all under control. Any new job is going to take several months to figure out. Hell, I remember when you started your clinic, I didn't see you for almost six months."

"I'm sorry," I whisper.

"I understood, darlin'," he replies, pouring our tea and joining me at the table. He takes my hand in his and gives it a squeeze. "Now, you need to be the one to show up and give him support while he gets this all sorted out. I'm not saying he did everything right, but I don't think you've taken a minute to walk in his shoes."

"No, I've been too busy missing him," I admit. "It's not easy to go from all of his attention to none of it."

"I know." He smiles softly. "Why do you think I've been so angry at your mama?"

"Oh, Dad." I cover our hands with my free one and feel tears spring to my eyes. "But it wasn't her fault."

"And I don't think this is Jace's fault either," he says. "I've decided to start sorting through your mom's things over the next few months. I'm going to have to take baby steps."

"We'll help," I promise him. "I'm proud of you, Dad."

"Your mom would have been so excited at the thought of being a grandma." His lip quivers with unshed tears. "She would have spoiled this baby like crazy."

"I know it." I nod and let my tears fall unchecked down my cheeks. "Seems I've been doing a lot of crying lately."

"Hormones," he says with a laugh. "I think you owe Jace an apology, Joy."

"Yeah." I swallow hard and pull away, leaning back in my seat. "I messed it all up."

"I'd say you both did a good job of that," he says before taking a sip of his tea. "This still tastes like twigs to me."

"Then why did you brew it?"

"Well, isn't that what you do for pregnant ladies? Make them tea?"

I dissolve into giggles, happy that I came home to see my dad. "I guess you do. I think it's good, thank you."

"Are you going to go find him after this?"

"No."

He scowls at me, and I shrug a shoulder. "I have a few things to do, but I'm going to text him and ask him to meet with me."

"That's what's wrong with you young people today," he says, shaking his head. "Just go find him, fling yourself at him, and say you're sorry."

"I don't see it unfolding that way."

"You always did have to make everything difficult," he grumbles.

"Thanks for the tough love."

"Keep me posted," he responds. "Now, I have to go finish tinkering with my truck."

"Want some help?"

He glances at me in surprise. "I could always use an extra pair of hands."

twenty

Jace

"You look like shit," Levi says after opening the door.

"I haven't slept," I admit, following him through his condo to the kitchen. "Did I wake you up?"

"I just got home myself," he replies. "Long night at work. Want some coffee?"

"Yes, please." I sit at his table, feeling hollow as I watch him move about the kitchen.

"How's the leg?"

"Fine," he says with a shrug, then watches me closely. "What's wrong?" he asks as he hands me my cup and sits across from me, watching me with tired eyes.

"Joy's pregnant," I begin and then laugh humorlessly. "Which I still haven't wrapped my head around."

"Congratulations."

I nod and take a sip of coffee. "We had a pretty big fight last night. Or, she did. I stood there and took it on the sidewalk because she wanted to yell at me."

"What for?"

"Not being around this past month. I told Joy I'd make her a priority, and work has been, well, insane."

"I see."

"To say she's angry is a huge understatement. In all fairness, I did show up to dinner about three hours late last night."

"Jace," he says in surprise, and I wince.

"I know. It wasn't cool. I just got caught up. I *always* get caught up, and it feels like a shit excuse, but it's the truth. Maybe I should give up the chief position."

Levi exhales loudly but doesn't say anything.

"Go ahead. Just say it."

"You'll resent her," he replies. "If you give up the position you busted your ass off for, you'll resent her. Maybe not today, but one day, you will. And that's not fair to either of you."

"I agree, but I don't see how to do this otherwise." I rap my fingers on the table in frustration. "Sixteen to twenty-hour days aren't conducive to a healthy relationship."

"Jesus, why are you working that many hours?"

"Because both positions are full-time," I reply with a sigh. "Now I understand why the hospital has gone through three chiefs of surgery over the past five years."

"Those are sweat-shop hours," Levi says, making me chuckle. "You can't have *any* life with that schedule."

"I know, and I'll do whatever it takes to fix it, but Joy was also unreasonable. I've never been so angry with her in my life." I rub the back of my neck. "She basically said that I'll be a shit father and husband and she's reconsidering marrying me."

"Isn't love fun?" Levi asks, laughing when I glare at him.

"Speaking of love, you've been pretty tight-lipped about the pop star."

"And it's staying that way."

"It's just us here," I remind him. "Why do you look angry every time she's mentioned?"

He stares at me, his grey eyes hot, and I don't think he's going to answer me at all.

"She ghosted me," he finally admits and then swears under his breath. "I feel fucking stupid."

"So you slept together, and then you never heard from her again?"

"Exactly."

I frown, the idea of anyone hurting my brother not sitting well with me.

"Was the sex that bad?"

"Fuck you."

I smirk. "Okay, so it was awesome. Good for you."

He just flips me off, and I hold my hands up in surrender. "Hey, I don't know what to say. Maybe it was just a one-night stand."

"Maybe." He sighs and scratches his head in irritation. "Do I sound like a fucking moron when I say that I felt like we had a connection?"

"You're not a moron. Maybe it scared her."

"Scared me," he says. "But damn if I could get enough of her. We didn't leave that hotel room for twenty-four hours."

"Damn. I'm impressed."

"So was she," he says with a grin, but the smile doesn't last long. "And then I tried to call her that night, and she didn't answer. She hasn't returned any of my calls or texts, although I stopped trying after the first week. I'm no stalker."

"That's good to hear. It sounds to me like it scared her, man. The sex was *too* good."

"That doesn't help me sleep at night, smartass."

"Maybe reach out to her in a month or so. Give her some space." I shrug helplessly. "What the hell do I know? My fiancée pretty much told me to eat shit and die last night."

"Maybe it was the hormones talking," he suggests.

"Her feelings are hurt, and that kills me," I reply. "I want to go to her house right now and make her hear me out."

"So, do it," he says.

"This is Joy we're talking about. I can't *make* her do anything. I need to get some stuff in order and then go to her with a plan."

"This could be interesting," Levi says. "What kind of a plan?"

"I'm too type A to not have a plan. And the truth is, I miss her, too. I don't want to go to her and have her reject me twice, I couldn't survive it again."

"What's the plan?" he asks again.

"I haven't figured that out yet. You tell me the plan."

"Dude, you're talking to a guy who had the best sex of his life with arguably the most famous woman in the world and can't get her to call him back. I don't think I'm the right person to ask about a plan."

I laugh and then shrug. "Well, then we're screwed."

"Wyatt seems to have it figured out. He got the girl. Let's call him."

"Is nine in the morning too early to start day-drinking? We could call him over and get drunk."

"Don't turn into that guy," Levi says. "No one wants to marry the day drinker. That's only funny in college."

"I didn't do it then, either," I remind us. "Joy would have told me I was a loser and never spoken to me again."

"She would have been right," he says. "She always was a smart girl."

"And tolerant. I admit that over the past couple of years I've only called her when I needed something, and I hate that I slipped back into that old habit over the past month, especially after promising her that I wouldn't do that."

"Cut yourself a little slack," he says. "You were trying to get your bearings after being suspended *and* starting a new position. That would take anyone some time."

"Yeah, but it would have only taken thirty seconds to return a text or a phone call." I blow out a breath. "I can do better than that."

I *have* to do better than that because I'm going to be a dad. Dad.

"Holy shit, I'm going to be a dad. I don't know anything about kids. What if I screw it up?"

Levi laughs. "You won't. You're going to be a wonderful father. Right after you start doing better."

"Agreed."

"You really haven't been much help."

He just laughs and flips me off again. "You drank my coffee and bitched about your troubles. What else did you want?"

"Just that, I suppose. Thanks, brother."

"Anytime."

"THANKS FOR MEETING me on such short notice," I say later in the afternoon, sitting before the board of directors of Seattle General.

"What's going on, Jace?" Mick asks.

The board is comprised of Mick and four other members, some doctors, and some administrators.

"I have a request," I begin. "I'd like to requisition the money to hire a full-time executive assistant."

"You have an assistant," Olive Sanders says, pursing her lips.

"And she does fine with my schedule, but I want someone with more experience and more expertise in medical practices. The person I want to hire won't come cheap, but I feel that it's important for my wellbeing."

"Go on," Edward Cussler says.

"Frankly, working close to twenty hours a day isn't working well for me. I love the position, and I know that I'm good at it, but bringing on a well-qualified executive assistant will help immensely with the amount of paperwork that I have every day, on top of the surgeries I still perform."

"Many chiefs choose to back off on their surgery loads," Edwards suggests, but I shake my head.

"That's exactly the opposite of what I want. I'm an excellent surgeon, and I hope that you agree that my primary function here should be in the operating room."

"We don't disagree with that," Mick says.

"And frankly, we don't want you here for twenty hours a day," Edward replies. "A burned-out doctor doesn't do anyone any good, and is dangerous. We need you to perform at the best of your ability. I don't see a problem with allocating the funds for a full-time assistant."

He rambles off a yearly salary budget that makes me smile. I even have someone in mind for the position, and they will gladly take that salary.

"I'm engaged, and I'm about to become a father," I tell them. "I know I don't have to tell you that, but I want to be as transparent as possible with you. While the hospital and our patients are incredibly important to me, so is my fiancée and our child. It's my hope that with the addition of my assistant, I can decrease to about twelve-hour days, barring any emergencies. Five days a week, of course."

"That sounds reasonable to me," Olive says. "Congratulations, Dr. Crawford."

"Thank you."

After discussing a few more specifics, I hurry back to my office to make some calls and get going on my way to balancing my life. I need to reschedule a couple of things, and actually delegate a few more, which isn't easy for a type-A personality like me, but it's absolutely necessary.

I shoot a text to Joy.

Can you please meet with me at my place this evening? Seven o'clock?

I grab my keys and am heading out the door when she replies.

I'll be there.

twenty-one

Joy

6:57.

I'm ridiculous.

This is *Jace*. He's my best friend and the love of my life, and I'm sitting outside in my SUV like a chickenshit.

There's no good reason to be scared, and yet, here I am, terrified.

I jump at the knock and put a hand to my chest as I roll the window down.

"What are you doing out here?" Jace asks. God, it's good to see him. His eyes are warm and eating me up like he's happy to see me, too.

I hope he's glad to see me. I wouldn't blame him if he gave me a piece of his mind and kicked me out after the way I acted last night.

"I'm waiting for seven," I reply and glance at the clock.

6:59.

"Come on." He opens my door, and I cut the engine, reach for my handbag, and get out of the car. He shuts the door and reaches for my hand, which fills me with so much relief I want to cry. "You don't ever wait outside, Joy. This is your home, too."

He ushers me inside and takes my coat. Once I've toed off my shoes, he takes my hand again and leads me into the living room.

With the arrival of fall, it gets dark so much earlier in the evening. But Seattle is lit up before us through the windows. He has the gas fireplace lit. It's long and filled with blue stones that glimmer from the light of the fire.

It's beautiful.

So, I stand in front of it, my arms wrapped around my middle while I try to pull my thoughts together.

"Joy, I'd like to talk."

"I know," I whisper. "I want to talk, too, I'm just trying to figure out what to say."

"Well, I'll start then. Please, come sit with me."

I turn and look at him, sitting on the edge of the couch with his arms resting on his legs, his hands hanging loosely between his knees. He watches me intently as if he's trying to see inside my head.

"I've had some time to think," he begins, and for the first time, it occurs to me that he might have asked me here to formally break up with me.

Fuck.

I take a deep breath and sit beside him, but before he says anything, he pins me against the couch and kisses the ever-loving hell out of me. His hands dive into my hair, holding on tightly as his lips caress mine, brushing back and forth until I'm a squirming pile of mush from wanting him.

When he pulls back for air, I breathe, "Wow."

"*This* is who we are, Joy. This is you and me. Always. Even when it's hard. When we fight and when we're happy. We love each other."

"I love you so much," I murmur, my voice cracking with emotion. "And I owe you the biggest apology in the history of apologies."

"Shh."

"No, it's true." I sit up, forcing him to back away and listen. "I'm *so sorry* for the way I spoke to you last night. It was the hurt talking, the surprise from finding out about the baby, and just . . . *everything*. I told you before that I'm proud of you, and I am. I'm *so damn proud*."

He reaches over and takes my hand in his, listening. "But then I turned around and punished you for being successful, and that's not fair. I promise to *never* do that to you again, Jace."

"Thank you. And I'm sorry that I've been MIA," he says, pulling my hand up to kiss my knuckles. "I've been overwhelmed, to say the least, but that's not an excuse for not communicating with you."

"We'll do better," I insist. "But I have more to apologize for. I'm sorry about the way I told you about the baby. I shouldn't have blurted it out like that in anger. When I found out yesterday, and then you invited me to dinner, I was excited to tell you at the restaurant."

"And then I was hours late, making you wait for me. That's not going to happen again, sweetheart. I promise."

"I was frustrated," I admit. "But again, not a good excuse. I sounded like a brat, and I'm sorry."

"I think that we've had a *lot* of life changes recently, and we're both trying to get our footing," he says, pushing my hair back behind my ear. "Are you happy about the baby?"

I smile, feeling my eyes fill with tears. "Yeah. I'm excited. I'd never really given motherhood much thought because I was always so career-driven, but now that it's happening, well, I don't think I could be happier."

"I'm so glad," he says, closing his eyes in relief. "I'm happy, too. And I know that my job isn't super conducive to being a good dad—"

"That's bullshit," I reply fiercely, "and I was horrible to throw that in your face."

"You weren't wrong," he says, frowning. "You should know that I've made some adjustments at work."

"You did *not* give up the chief position." I feel myself going pale at the thought, but he shakes his head no.

"No, I don't think I could. I worked too hard for it, Joy. But I did hire an excellent executive assistant who's going to come on and take over the majority of the paperwork and scheduling. I'm hoping to whittle my work hours down to no more than twelve hours a day, five days a week. Here."

He reaches for a book on the coffee table and opens it up.

"A planner?" I ask and then laugh. "I should have known. Only you, Dr. Crawford."

"Hey, I'm organized," he says with a smile. "This is for both of us. I've already written in what my schedule looks like for the next month. As you can see, the next two weeks are still very busy because I'm training my new assistant, but it starts to open up a bit after that."

"You've written in *love weekends* twice a month." I trace the words written in Jace's chicken-scratch with my fingertips.

"That's right," he says. "And I'll do my best to be home at the same time as you in the evenings, as long as there's not an emergency that needs my attention."

"Jace, this is just . . . I don't have words."

"Well, there's more. As we get closer to the baby coming, and we have a clearer picture of the due date, I'll arrange to take the two weeks off starting the day you give birth. I *want* to be here with both of you."

"You're amazing," I whisper, then point to next Wednesday. "Can you pencil me in here for lunch? I'll come meet you at the hospital."

"Of course." He writes it in with a smile. "We will schedule vacations and time together in advance. And I'll do my best to make my schedule mirror yours as much as I can."

"Thank you." I set the book on the table and climb into his lap, framing his face in my hands. "Thank you so much for doing this."

"We are going to make this work," he promises. "And I owe you an apology, too. I promised that I wouldn't make you feel like you're second-fiddle to my job, and I didn't succeed in that endeavor. Joy, I can't promise that I won't still work a lot, but I can guarantee that I'll try harder, and do everything I can to respect our schedule."

"Thank you," I repeat, resting my forehead against his. "What do we do now?"

"Get naked," he suggests.

"No." I giggle and press my lips to his in a quick kiss. "I mean, what do we do next? I don't want to get married when I'm huge."

"I'm quite sure we can pull together a wedding before that happens. We have time. First, though, where are we going to live?"

I blink, not having thought of that before. "Oh, good point. It would make sense to live here. It's bigger than my house and closer to your job."

"I don't want you to have to commute far for *your* job," he says with a frown.

"Well, I have some work news, too. With the baby coming, I don't think I'll want to go back full-time. I'm hoping for three days one week, four the next, and then alternate that way."

"I love that idea," he says. "But you own the business."

"I'll still own it, I'm just going to hire another part-time doctor. I have time to find the right fit."

"Well, since we're on the same page about where we'll live, follow me."

He stands with me in his arms, sets me on the floor, and leads me through the house to the bedroom next to the master. It's just a normal-sized room with a small walk-in closet, currently housing some home gym equipment.

"How do you feel about this room as the nursery?"

"Hmm." I tap my finger on my lips. "It's going to need some paint."

His lips twitch, and his eyes shine in happiness. "I know a girl."

"Nah-ah," I say, shaking my head. "I don't think pregnant women are supposed to be around the fumes."

"Good point. I'll hire someone."

"Then I think it's the perfect room for the baby."

Suddenly, I'm scooped up into his arms, and he's marching into our bedroom.

"Now what are you doing?"

"Well, since all of our business is sorted, I'm getting you naked. Any objections?"

"Not even one."

epilogue

Joy

Five years later . . .

"Mama!" Elizabeth Grace comes running over the wet sand toward me, her hand stretched out, and her sweet face lit up with excitement. "Mama, look!"

"What do you have there, pumpkin?"

"A crab!"

She reaches me and gingerly holds a tiny, squirming crab in her hand.

"Yes, you do. This is a hermit crab."

I spend a couple of minutes explaining how I know that, and then she's off again to put the crab back in the water.

My four-year-old is a sponge, soaking up everything in the entire world that she can. She loves animals like her mama, and she's so damn smart, just like her daddy. We named her Elizabeth, after my mother, and I'll never forget the day she was born, and my dad heard her name for the first time.

It might have been one of the few times I've seen him cry.

"This one is sleepy," Jace says as he returns from his walk down the beach. He's carrying our six-month-old son in a baby carrier. "If you'd like to take him back to the condo, I'll play with Lizzy for a bit and then join you for lunch."

"I like that plan." Before I take Elijah from him, I rise up on my tiptoes for a kiss. Jace cups my ass and gives it a squeeze.

"I don't want to give everyone a show out here," he murmurs against my lips. His eyes are full of mischief.

"We'll put on our own show later," I assure him, taking the sleeping baby from him. "See you in a bit."

We bought the condo in Maui two years ago when we decided that we needed another investment opportunity, *and* a place to get away from it all. We come at least four times a year.

"Mama!" I stop at the foot of our steps and turn in surprise. Lizzy is running toward me, her face deep in concentration. Jace is right behind her.

"What is it?"

"You just *left* us!"

"I left you with Daddy so I could put Elijah down for a nap. I thought you'd want to play some more."

She shakes her head and climbs right up the steps ahead of me.

"We go together," she informs us. "As a family."

I glance at Jace, who just shrugs and takes the baby from me, cuddling him against his chest. "I guess she told us. She's bossy. Like her mama."

I snort, following my whole life up the steps to our home in paradise.

It's a good life. It's a very good life.

Enjoy an excerpt from

STAY
with me

A *With Me In Seattle* Novel

prologue

Amelia

"You've got to be kidding me."

I sit and stare at my attorney, watching her thin, painted-pink lips move, but I'm definitely not understanding what the hell she's saying, because I'm pretty sure she just said "your divorce isn't actually final" and that just can't be right.

It can't fucking be right.

"—sorry."

She's folded her hands over my file on her desk and is looking at me with sympathetic, blue eyes.

"I apologize, Pam," I begin and shift in my seat. "You're going to have to repeat that because I think you just said that I'm *not* divorced, and that can't be right."

"That's what I said," Pam replies with a nod. "He contested."

He motherfucking contested.

"I sat in a courtroom two months ago, and a judge granted the divorce. I have signed papers."

"I know," Pam says with a nod. "But because he didn't appear in court, and he wasn't pleased with the settlement amount, his lawyer filed contest papers, and the judge granted it."

"This is bullshit."

"I don't disagree with you."

"I worked for *two years* to make this divorce happen, Pam." Two years of panic attacks. Two years of stress. Two years of worrying, every single day, that this divorce would never happen, after five years of mental and emotional abuse. I'm done.

"I know, I've been with you for those two years."

I sit back and stare at her, struck numb. "What now?"

"Well, you'll have to either go through mediation and reach a settlement between you, or we go to court. Again."

"Jesus," I mutter and rub my fingertips over my forehead, trying to wipe away the headache that seems to be permanently housed behind my eyes. "He's trying to suck me dry. This is just about the money, Pam. He's not trying to keep me, or save a marriage that has no chance in hell of being saved."

"I agree with that, as well." Pam sighs and reads over the letter I received from the court for the third time. "We're going to get this handled, Lia."

"I know." I blow out a breath, determined not to cry. I will not give Vincent Borgen another tear. Ever. "So, what now?"

"I want to have him served with failure to appear papers, and I have a hunch that he'll have you served with lawsuit papers."

"A lawsuit?" I stare at her, again, as if she's grown a second nose. "What in the hell could he possibly sue me for?"

"Oh, about a dozen things, all just to make this process more painful and slow." She leans forward again. "So, here's what I want you to do. Get out of town."

"You want me to leave L.A?"

"Immediately," she says with a nod. "We want him to be served first, and I don't want you to be served at all. In the meantime, I'm going to take care of this here."

"Where am I going to go?" I frown. "I guess I could go to my parents' in Seattle."

"No." She shakes her head. "Your parents' address is on record, and they'll try to have you served there. Go to Seattle if you want, but don't stay with them."

"For fuck's sake," I mutter and go back to rubbing my forehead. "Okay, I have other family I can call."

"Good."

"This is really bad timing. I'm launching my new makeup brand next month, and all of my meetings are in L.A."

"I'm sorry," she says and finally offers me a small smile. "I truly am. I know this is inconvenient and just mean on his part."

"Typical. He's got a mean streak the size of Texas." I rub my forehead again. "I can't believe I'm not divorced from the jerk."

"We'll get it figured out. For now, go on vacation for a while, and I'll keep you posted as to what's happening here. If I need you to appear, we'll arrange it."

"Okay."

"And, Lia, you will want to postpone the launch of your brand. Making that kind of money when you aren't divorced yet will only complicate things."

"And he could get a cut of it."

"He could."

Mother fucker.

"Understood. I'll be in touch."

I walk out of her office and to my car, where I sit and stare unblinkingly at the traffic driving by.

Did that just happen? Am I dreaming?

I pinch myself and then frown at the pain. Not dreaming.

So, I need to go somewhere. Not to my parents'. I'm certainly not going to stay with my brother. Archer has more women coming in and out of his bedroom than, well, anyone should. Gross.

And my sister, Anastasia, is just getting ready to move to Seattle for her new job. She is way too busy to add this to her plate.

I bite my lip and pick up my phone, remembering what my cousin Jules said the last time I saw her. That if I ever need anything, all I have to do is call.

Here's hoping she meant it.

She answers on the third ring.

"Hello. Oh crap, hold on." She pulls the phone away from her ear. "Nate, can you take that away from Stella? She could kill herself with that."

I smile, the sound of her voice making me feel a little better.

"Sorry," Jules says. "Toddlers are adorable when they sleep. When they're awake, they're little terrors."

"She's a beautiful terror," I remind her.

"True. What's up, Lia?"

"I need your help." I clear my throat. "I need a place to stay."

"What's going on?"

I fill her in on the divorce, and how I'm suddenly *not* divorced, and how my attorney wants me to lay low for a while.

"I know it's a lot to ask, but I can't stay with my folks, and I don't like the idea of my name being on a lease somewhere. He'll just figure out where I am."

"I never liked him," she mutters, and I can only nod in

agreement. "We will figure this out."

"Are you sure? I know you have a lot on your plate, and I don't want to make things difficult."

"Oh, girl, this is not difficult. You get your beautiful self up here, and we will get you settled. I think I already know of a great place, I just have to call Natalie. Oh, and I'll talk Nate out of kicking Vinnie's ass."

"He can kick his ass. I don't have an issue with that."

Jules laughs, and I hear a commotion in the background. "Shit. I have to go. Just text me when you have details."

She hangs up, and I immediately begin making plans to fly to Seattle.

Today.

one

Amelia

"**A**re you kidding me?" I'm standing in the middle of a beautiful home that has views of Puget Sound, an open-concept living room and kitchen, and a freaking *pool* in the backyard. "When you said that you'd find me a place, I didn't expect this."

"Oh, trust me, I'm not kidding," Jules says and nods, like it's no big deal. "Natalie and I used to live here when we were single. Then Brynna and Caleb lived here for a while, but now that they've moved into their place out in Bellevue, it's just been sitting empty."

"Nat and Luke talked about selling," Nate adds. Jules' husband is something to write home about. I can't look directly at him, or I might embarrass all of us by drooling. With his long hair, dark features, and the sleeve tattoos, he might be every woman's wet dream. "But they haven't yet, so it's the perfect place for you to crash for a while."

"And the best part is, your name isn't anywhere on it," Jules agrees as she slips her hand into her husband's, linking their fingers. "You can stay here as long as you need to."

"You've bought me furniture," I point out, still in awe as men carry couches, tables, and beds up the stairs. "This is insane."

"It was empty because Brynna and Caleb moved out," Jules says with a frown. "You can't sleep on the floor."

"You bought me furniture," I repeat as if she didn't hear me.

"You're family," Jules says. "So there's really nothing else to discuss. Do you want me to have one of Nate's minions bring in groceries?"

"His minions?" I raise a brow, and Jules laughs.

"Inside joke," she says and smiles up at her husband.

"I can make a call," Nate says, but I shake my head no.

"I can call Uber Eats for that, or order with any grocery store and pick it up. The internet is a beautiful thing."

"You're sure? Nate has people." Jules tilts her head, watching me with our signature Montgomery blue eyes.

"Me, too." I hold up my phone for them to see and smile. "Really, I'm great. This is *so great.*" I feel tears threaten, but before they can fall, Jules wraps me up in her slim arms and holds me close.

"I'm so happy you're here. Take time to settle in. Luke's already called to have the internet hooked back up, and the Wi-Fi info is on the kitchen counter." She backs away and bites her lip as she looks around. "I think that's it, but if you need anything, just call. We're not far, and Luke's right up the street."

"Where's Natalie?"

"Oh, she's around too, but she had a baby about six weeks ago, so Luke keeps her tucked away." Jules rolls her eyes, and Nate just grins. "Luke's a little protective."

"That's kind of sweet."

"It's their fourth baby, Lia." Jules shakes her head. "He's turned her into a baby factory."

"They're quite happy," Nate says and then leans in to kiss Jules' cheek. "And Luke insists they're finished at four children."

"*Four* kids?" I ask. How in the world did I not know that they now have four kids? "Wow, I guess I haven't been home in a while."

And that just makes me sad, and angry at Vinnie all over again. I wanted to move home years ago, and he wasn't having it.

"You haven't," Jules says. "But you're home now, and I hope we get to see plenty of you."

"That would be great."

"We should let her get settled," Nate says. "Here are the keys to Julianne's little red Lexus."

"You do not have to give me your car," I insist. "I can rent one."

"It's really no biggie," Jules says. "I don't use the Lexus much anymore because it's too small for Stella's booster seat. It should get driven."

"Thank you. And thanks for letting me crash at your condo for a couple of days."

"It was our pleasure," Jules replies. "But you'll be happier here. It's hard to live with kids that aren't yours."

"Stella is beautiful."

"And a handful." Nate shrugs. "She's four."

We walk toward the door, and Nate stops and looks down at me. The man is *tall*.

"Lock this door, Lia. Always."

"I will." He's so *intense*.

"And set the alarm."

"Yes, sir." I smirk up at him, and he just smiles.

"Typical Montgomery woman, aren't you? Sarcastic as hell."

"Thank you." I drop into a curtsey and make them both laugh. "Don't worry, I'll lock up. But I think I'm fairly safe here."

"You are," Jules says as she waves and they leave, walking out to their black Mercedes SUV. The Lexus is parked in front of them, gleaming in the warm summer sunshine. It's going to be a pleasure to drive that little convertible around town. It takes the sting out of missing my own Mercedes in L.A.

I wave them off and walk back inside, obediently locking the door behind me. I guess if I have to be away from home for an unknown length of time, this isn't a bad place to do it in. It's great to be back in Seattle, where I know my family is just a phone call away if I need them.

Jules and Nate didn't have to buy this furniture. I could have done that, but they wanted to, and now I don't know how I'll repay them.

Not that they want me to repay them.

I shake my head and walk up the stairs to my bedroom. It has a killer view of the water and an en-suite bathroom with a long countertop, which is perfect for all of my makeup. I'll use the other bathroom on this floor to store the deliveries that I receive and to go through and decide which products I want to try and which I want to give away.

My job is fucking amazing.

Just when I get my suitcases unpacked and stored in the guest room, the doorbell rings, and everything in me stills.

Well, everything except my heart, which is beating out of my chest.

"It's just someone at the door," I remind myself. "It's probably not a process server. It's probably just a delivery."

Once down the stairs, I peek out a side window and find a man standing in front of the door. He's tall, with sunglasses covering his eyes. His dark hair is long. Not as long as Nate's, but he could use a haircut.

He's wearing a hoodie in the colors of Seattle's football team, and cargo shorts, which makes me frown.

If he's cold, why is he wearing shorts?

But the most important thing is, his hands are empty.

I open the door, only wide enough for one eye to peer outside.

"Yes?"

"Hi." He takes off his sunglasses and offers me a smile. "I'm Wyatt Crawford, your neighbor from across the way." He points to the large, white house behind him.

"Okay."

He tilts his head to one side. "I just saw the furniture being moved in here earlier and wanted to introduce myself."

"Great. Thanks." I move to shut the door, but he stops me.

"What's your name?"

"Look, Wyatt, I don't have any sugar or flour or extra eggs."

"I'm not baking."

"And I don't want any cookies."

"Not selling."

"And I don't need to find Jesus."

"Last I checked, He wasn't lost."

Okay, that makes my lips twitch, but I hold firm.

"Thanks for coming over to say hi. I have stuff to do." And with that, I shut the door and lock it. I lean my back against the wood and shut my eyes. I'm not a rude woman. But I am unnerved, and my guard is up, and I'm here alone.

Not to mention, I don't trust men.

I peek out the side window to see Wyatt walking down the driveway toward his house, and I head back upstairs, ready to get my makeshift studio set up in the guest bedroom.

I may not trust men, but the neighbor is handsome. Not that I'm in the market for a handsome man—or any man for that matter.

"IF TODAY'S VIDEO helped you, please give it a like below, and don't forget to click that subscribe button to be a part of the Beauty Brigade, my friends. I'll be back next week with something new. Before I see you again, remember that the most beautiful part about you is what's inside of you. We're just polishing up the outside. Have a great week, everyone."

I smile as I hit end on the camera and sit back to look through the video to make sure there's nothing that I need to film over again.

I'll splice it together tomorrow and get it ready to publish on YouTube on Friday.

I've made quite the name for myself as a beauty and fashion vlogger. With more than three million followers on YouTube, and close to two million on Instagram, I have an impressive following.

All because I love makeup and pretty clothes.

I've been told that the camera loves me, which is a bonus.

Now, I've been approached by one of the biggest makeup

and skincare retailers in the country to formulate my own makeup brand. It's almost ready to launch, but I'm stuck in this holding pattern. Again.

I thought it was over. I thought I could finally move forward with my life and leave my past where it belongs.

Instead, I'm waiting. Just like I have been for more than two years.

It's ridiculous.

I shake my head as I wrap up the video, turn off the lights, and carry my makeup brushes into the bathroom to clean them and get them ready for the next recording.

The doorbell rings, and I roll my eyes, hopeful that Mr. Neighbor hasn't decided that he needs a cup of sugar, after all. But it's not Wyatt, it's the UPS man with a delivery.

Day one, and the deliveries have already caught up to me. Which is fantastic.

I unbox the goodies from It cosmetics, and log the foundations, powders, and brushes into my spreadsheets. I keep track of everything that arrives, whether I've ordered it or if it's a freebie from the company. I also keep track of if I try it, use it in a video or on Instagram, and what I think of the product.

With dozens of things arriving each week, there's just no other way to keep track of everything. Not to mention, it feeds my organized soul.

My phone pings with a text from Jules.

If you're free, I'm bringing Natalie and wine over at 6pm. Sit by the pool?

I grin, excited to see them both, and reply. *Yes! Yay! I'll order pizza.*

I check the clock. I have two hours until they arrive. It's

the perfect amount of time to get in some yoga and a shower.

Just as I'm about to step under the hot spray, Jules texts back. *Awesome. See you soon!*

"I HAVEN'T TOLD my parents that I'm here yet," I confide to Nat and Jules a few hours later. We're sitting by the pool in the backyard, lounging on the most comfortable outdoor chairs I've ever sat in, sipping our wine.

We've already decimated the pizza.

"They won't be happy," Jules says, exchanging a look with Natalie, who looks fucking amazing for just having had a baby.

"I know." I sigh, watching the water in the pool. "It sucks. My family has been under enough stress because of my divorce. I finally thought it was over, and we all celebrated. With a party. How do I say *'oops! Never mind!'*"

"I wouldn't say it like that," Natalie replies with a laugh.

"I know for a fact that Uncle Stan and Aunt Sherri would be totally supportive and angry on your behalf." Jules takes a sip of her wine.

"I know. I'll call them tomorrow." I fidget with the button on the cushion of my chair. "Thanks for everything, Jules."

"You've thanked me about forty times."

"Well, I'm thanking you again. And you, too, Nat. Thanks for letting me stay here. It's so beautiful, and perfect for what I need. I set up a studio in the upstairs guest room for my videos."

"Oh, perfect," Nat says with a smile. She might be one of the most beautiful people I've ever met. With long, dark hair, green eyes, and a calm soul, she's always made me feel comfortable around her. "I want you to be at ease here. Well, as at ease as you can, given the circumstances. And if you need anything, Luke and I are just up the road a ways."

"Thanks." I blow out a breath. "Honestly, I'm a bit surprised that you're both so willing to help. Not because I think you're mean or anything, but, Jules, you're a bit older than me, and we've never been close. I always looked up to you."

"Well, when I was twenty, and you were fifteen, I probably didn't want you around," Jules admits with a laugh. "But you're an adult, and you're my cousin. I'm always happy to help. I would love to see more of you. I think we have a lot in common."

"I watch your videos every week," Natalie adds. "I get a lot of great tips from you."

"Me, too," Jules says with a nod. "We're girly girls, through and through."

"I love that," I reply. "I'd love to go shopping with you guys."

"Hallelujah," Natalie says, throwing her hands into the air. "I've been pregnant forever, and now that Chelsea is a couple months old, I can leave her for a few hours at a time. So, yes. Please, let's go shopping soon."

"We could invite all of the girls," Jules says, her brain working. "Make it a shopping day-slash-girls' night out."

"Oh, yes," Nat says, nodding vigorously. "You probably haven't had a chance to get to know everyone."

"I haven't been home since Dom's wedding."

"That was three years ago," Jules says. "We definitely need to get all the girls together."

"Awesome." I high five both of them, excited to spend time with all of my cousins and their significant others "Hey, I've been meaning to ask, what's in that building?" I ask, pointing to the small structure behind the house.

"My studio," Natalie says. "Just so you know, I'll be in and out sometimes with clients, but we'll walk around the house. I take photos in there."

"Oh, how fun."

"I should do some photos for you," Nat says. "You're absolutely stunning."

"She does boudoir photos," Jules warns me.

"Actually, I could use a bunch of shots for my new brand. I can't be in L.A. for the sessions, but I bet we could do them here."

"I'd be happy to," Natalie says, her face lighting up with a smile. "Just let me know what you need, and we'll make it happen."

"Thank you. I could also use some shots for social media. I had a girlfriend in L.A. who did those for me, but—"

"Say no more," Natalie says, holding up a hand. "I'm your girl, and I'm ready to get back to work part-time. Let's set something up for later in the week."

"This is amazing." I stare at both of them as they smile back at me. Wide, happy smiles. It feels so good to be back with family. "I can't wait."

"Me either," Natalie says.

"I want to come, too," Jules adds.

"I wouldn't have it any other way."

Stay With Me is Available Now

CPSIA information can be obtained
at www.ICGtesting.com
Printed in the USA
LVHW031032281118
598372LV00019B/347